JOSEPH McGEE PRIVATE INVESTIGATOR

THE
INTERN MURDERS
McGee's Foray into the World of High
Crimes and Secret Society Killers

BY
CARL DOUGLASS
Neurosurgeon Turned Author Writes With
Gripping Realism

PUBLICATION
CONSULTANTS
We Believe In The Power Of Authors

PO Box 221974 Anchorage, Alaska 99522-1974
books@publicationconsultants.com—www.publicationconsultants.com

ISBN Number: 978-1-63747-108-1
eBook ISBN Number: 978-1-63747-109-8

Library of Congress Number: 2023936825

Manufactured in the United States of America

DISCLAIMER

All the novellas in the McGee Series, especially Book Ten, are works of fiction and should not be construed as representing real persons, places, or events. Some names of real persons and places appear but only for the purpose of creating a setting in the real world or as a mention of historical circumstances. None of the real people or the real places were actually involved in the fictional portrayals found in these short books.

DEDICATION

To my ever faithful family

CHAPTER
ONE

The first Monday in October is a month and day of singular importance to a select group of Americans. Most of the rest of the population of the country is hardly aware of what is taking place. That day is the opening of the Supreme Court of the United States–known familiarly as SCOTUS–which is the highest court in the federal judiciary of the United States of America. It has ultimate *appellate jurisdiction* over all federal and state court cases that involve a point of federal law, and original jurisdiction over a narrow range of cases, specifically "all Cases affecting Ambassadors, other public Ministers and Consuls, and those in which a State shall be Party".

The Court holds the power of judicial review–the ability to invalidate a statute for violating a provision of the Constitution. It is also able to strike down presidential directives for violating either the Constitution or statutory law. However, it may act only within the context of a case in an area of law over which it has jurisdiction. The Court may decide cases having political overtones, but it has ruled that it does not have power to decide non-justiciable political questions.

Through its long history, its actions have been largely discretionary, contrary to the assumption of many Americans that the justices know the Constitution backwards and forwards with all its nuances; and because of the great combined judicial knowledge and wisdom found on the court, it can and should, determine the true and original founding fathers' meaning as contained in the Constitution.

The court is easily the most powerful unelected body in America, and the members are appointed for life. They cannot be removed by anything but an extraordinary act of impeachment. Only once in the 232 years since its establishment has any sitting justice been impeached. That was Justice Samuel Chase in 1805. The House of Representatives passed Articles of Impeachment against him on March 12, 1804. He had been accused of refusing to dismiss biased jurors and of excluding or limiting defense witnesses in two politically sensitive cases; however–the following year–he was acquitted by the Senate.

It was into that exalted and ultimately secure position that Daniel George Cabot III entered as its Chief Justice to be sworn in as the first order of business of the court. He was a hide-bound Republican; and a patrician Harvard undergraduate, who held a juris doctor degree from the same Ivy League institution; and who had the perfect path to his seat at the head of the table.

In law school, he was the top of his class, editor of the Harvard Law Review, and then was selected as clerk for the inimitable, blunt, irascible, man, Associate Justice Byron White from Arizona. After his clerkship, Cabot entered the federal judiciary by being appointed to the district [trial] bench in the southern district of New York.

Chief Justice Hughes said of the Judges of The Southern District of New York, "The Courts are what the judges make them, and the District Court in New York, from the time of [District Judge] James Duane, [President] Washington's first appointment, has had a special distinction by reason of the outstanding abilities of the men who have been called to its service."

Many of the new Chief Justice's fellow judges and the attorneys who argued before him said that he could well be one of those whom Chief Justice Hughes had in mind. After his stellar performance in New York, he was elevated to the position of judge in Chicago's 7th Circuit Court of Appeals, where he distinguished himself as the furthest to the right of any man in the federal court system and was known in the press as the Hanging Appeal Judge. With very little argument, he was considered to be the best and brightest of the conservative judiciary at any level even by his liberal detractors.

He established his bona fides as a premier conservative theorist in over two hundred arcane legal papers he wrote before he was forty-five. He was the hanging low-fruit for picking when the most recent highly conservative populist president, Irving David Duke, nominated him to succeed liberal Justice Catherine D. Levitt who died during a heated debate over abortion. He passed the advice and consent of the Senate with a 100% positive vote by the Senate GOP and without a single Democrat vote.

The new chief justice made in known that he wished to be known as Chief Justice Cabot III. He studied supreme court history, procedure, practice, decorum, and privilege, with dedication. On that first day of his life-time tenure on the court, he met with his associate justices in-camera to discuss the pending cases and to determine a preliminary order of hearing those cases.

As is customary in American courts, the nine Justices were seated by seniority around the conference table. New Chief Justice, Cabot III walked directly to his assigned seat and occupied the center chair; the senior Associate Justice took his seat to the Chief's right, the second senior to his left, and so on, alternating right and left by seniority. Cabot III made it clear that this formality would be observed for the duration of his tenure in the office.

A server brought in a tray of coffee, tea, water, and juice.

"Set it in front of me," Cabot III said, then brusquely told her, "exit the room, and see to it that no one else enters the room until we finish. Is that understood?"

"Perfectly, Sir. Shall I have the Court Police Officers stand in front of the door?"

"Yes."

She gave a small bow, turned, and walked out.

"Greetings to all of the associate justices. The first order of business will be to swear me in as Chief Justice. As you know, After Senate confirmation, the President signs a commission appointing the nominee—in this case, me–

who then must take two oaths before executing the duties of the office. These oaths are known as the Constitutional Oath and the Judicial Oath. I state that for the purpose of the record."

A special stenographer for the investiture sat in her recorder's chair and took copious notes in the peculiar hieroglyphic shorthand they use. Otherwise, no direct records were allowed to be kept of any kind.

"Furthermore," Chief Justice Cabot III said, "Administration of the Oaths of Office are left to the discretion of the Chief Justice, since neither the Constitution nor the Judiciary Act of 1789, specified the manner of administration of the oaths. The first Chief Justice, John Jay, said, 'No particular person being designated by Law, to administer to us the oaths prescribed by the Statute, I thought it best to take them before the Chief Justice of this state [New York].'

"Early members of the Court took their oaths before various government officials, including one early associate whose oath was administered by the then sitting mayor of Philadelphia. By my choice, I shall have my esteemed father, CEO of Cabot LLC corporation, deacon of the Episcopal Church, and past congressman serving the state of Massachusetts."

He stood up from his seat, walked to the large double doors of the conference room, and admitted the handsome white-haired gentleman who was dressed in a tuxedo for the occasion. Except for a few side glances among the associates, and some very very careful smiles, none of the men or women on the court hazarded an opinion, even by facial expression. A professional videographer and a photographer followed the chief justice and his august and well-known father into the room. For the associates, this was a first.

Cabot III said, "There has been a tradition wherein either the Chief Justice or the senior Associate Justice administered the Constitutional Oath. Since it would be too Napoleonic for me to 'crown' myself even though I am the "first among equals", my esteemed father will do that here and now in my place and in the place of our important senior Associate Justice, the honorable Judge Zysteric. For the second—the Judicial Oath—we will have Senior Associate Justice Mr. Zysteric read it here before the cameras and play that in the open court session later in the day when I take my seat on the Bench."

Two attendants carried the historic mahogany bench chair used by Chief Justice John Marshall from 1819 to 1835 into the room and placed it behind the Chief Justice-to-be, and he sat down in a regal pose.

"Representative Gerald William Henry Cabot II will now administer the oath," his son said.

He faced his father from the impressive throne-like chair wearing a bland formal expression. The room fell silent.

Cabot II's stentorian voice instructed his son to repeat after him,

"*I, Daniel George Cabot III, do solemnly swear (and affirm) that I will support and defend the Constitution of the United States against all enemies, foreign and domestic; that I will bear true faith and allegiance to the same; that*

I take this obligation freely, without any mental reservation or purpose of evasion; and that I will well and faithfully discharge the duties of the office on which I am about to enter. So help me God."

The new Chief Justice gave no explanation, but ordered the historic chair removed from the room and stood to face Senior Associate Justice, Mr. Angus Dagon Zysteric.

"Repeat the Judicial Oath after me, Judge Zysteric intoned."

"*I, Daniel George Cabot III, do solemnly swear (and affirm) that I will administer justice without respect to persons, and do equal right to the poor and to the rich, and that I will faithfully and impartially discharge and perform all the duties incumbent upon me under the Constitution. So help me God."*

Judge Nichols rolled her eyes at her fellow liberal, Judge Hays, otherwise there was no further acknowledgment of what every justice in the room believed to be hubristic chutzpah.

Now that he was obviously and constitutionally in charge of the Court, Chief Justice Cabot III began to put his stamp on the Court.

"Let us now go to the private conference room and determine our course of action overall. We need to have a plan and a direction, my father stressed that piece of wisdom vigorously. I also had the privilege of doing a law school internship under the late great prosecuting attorney, Randolph Gigliangi, the US Attorney for the Southern District of New York.

I am justifiably proud of our record in bringing down the mob and elevating the very concept of law-and-order. We made successful inroads into insider trader, Ponzi schemes, and violent crime in the ghettos of the large eastern cities. There is a severe imbalance in the legal processes as they apply to good patriotic Americans and the darlings of the progressive liberals. It is time to rectify that situation as much as this Court can."

The meeting was being conducted in strict secrecy as were all private gatherings of the Court for SCOTUS business. Not even staffers were allowed in the room.

"Among my mentors was Judge Carlsson when he was an attorney general in the same district as I later served, and now we serve together on the highest court in our beloved country. Even such a staunch conservative AG in his earlier years as Judge Douglass Carlsson, originally from Virginia, a good Southern Evangelical Christian, a former professor of law at University of Pennsylvania, and the editor of *The American Conservative Magazine*–a highly respected and objective news and opinion monthly–and now on the Court, had done internships with Gigliangi.

"Now, it saddens me to recognize that the man for whom I had real reverence and who had been the attorney for the best president in American history, has expressed public concern about the former president's attorney and field man. What are we to do? I ask you, what are we to do from this Court? Watch our progress in the days to come."

CHAPTER

TWO

Glen Lincoln Dastrup and Neal Crenshaw Gabler grew up together in the exclusive West Cambridge (Huron) Village, Massachusetts, population 4,200 at the time. Their neighborhood included some of the highest real estate and rental prices in Massachusetts. The top employers were Harvard University, and MIT. The most common family income exceeded $200,000 in 1977, the year they were both born. Huron was situated directly north of Boston, across the Charles River. Nearby, the MIT Campus (Area 2) is bordered on the north by Broadway, on the south and east by the Charles River, and on the west by the Grand Junction Railroad tracks.

Both boys were educated in Buckingham Browne & Nichols School, often referred to as BB&N–an independent co-educational day school in Cambridge, Massachusetts–from pre-kindergarten through fifth grade. From BB&N, they went on for grades 6-8 to CSUS [Cambridge Street Upper School, 850 Cambridge St, Cambridge, MA] another of the most prestigious schools in the USA. Their world and associations were gradually increasing in accordance with the long-term plans by their ambitious parents.

The boys met the rigid and very competitive requirements to enter the best high school in the United States which could compete for that status anywhere in the world. PEA [Phillips Exeter Academy] was co-founded by John and Elizabeth Phillips in 1781, who believed every student should have access to the very best education–one that embraces the ideals of both goodness and knowledge, although not strongly inclusive of humility.

PEA had a coeducational residential school with more than 1,000 high school students from the US and 33 foreign countries. Exeter has a centuries-old tradition of academic excellence and a commitment to empowering Exonians to find their place in the world, and that was the Supreme Court of the United States for the two bright and eager young men and their unflinchingly ambitious parents, who were also the strongest public relations firms for their two scions.

Most SCOTUS desirous young people come from Harvard first, and Yale second. For the Dastrup and Gabler families, third rank was not a consideration. They applied, lobbied, did favors, wrote preliminary letters to justices, and found unobtrusive ways to make friends with interns working for conservative justices. Liberal ideology in any of its forms was unthinkable for the blue-bloods, their extended families, their prestigious histories, and— consequently for their sons.

Harvard it was. Their hard educational work and achievements, their generous familial gifts to the right charities–i.e., the ones favored by the conservative justices—and their cultivation of the correct exclusive men's clubs, paid off in spades. Glen and Neal were both accepted to the educational institution from which the great majority of future justices came. It was rumored that the boys were the numbers one and two picks, but that was never clearly substantiated, nor was any reliable information ever made available about which young man was first, and which was second. It mattered very little, anyway, since both were overly prepared to matriculate at Harvard—if such a thing is even possible. They were destined to be the foremost DARs in their class, and objects of envy, some enmity, and a serious amount of fawning friend-shipping.

Harvard prestige, fame, and world-class networking, such as joining and becoming active in the Christ Church Cambridge, the *Episcopal Church* in *Harvard Square*, were worth every dime and hour the families spent—after full-tuition scholarships, the two young men earned the remainder of each of their four years of making their way through the complicated and vigorous competition of their undergraduate educations.

Harvard University was 140 years-old at the time of the American Revolution, and 245 years-old by the time the two young men–who were born with silver spoons in their mouths–graduated summa cum laude, and shared the honor of being co-valedictorians.

They were widely expected to join the ranks of such notable alumni—as: Harvard Law School affiliates and editors of the *Harvard Law Review* who became associate or chief justices of the Supreme Court [in chronological order of attendance at Harvard Law School].

Benjamin Robbins Curtis, 1832
Horace Gray, 1849
Melville Weston Fuller, Chief Justice, 1854-1855
Henry Billings Brown, 1859
Oliver Wendell Holmes, Jr., 1866
William Henry Moody, 1876-1877
Louis Dembitz Brandeis, 1877
Edward Terry Sanford, 1889
Felix Frankfurter, 1906
Harold Hitz Burton, 1912
William Joseph Brennan, Jr., 1931
Harry Andrew Blackmun, 1932
Lewis Franklin Powell, Jr., 1932
Ruth Bader Ginsburg, 1956-1958
Antonin Scalia, 1960
Anthony McLeod Kennedy, 1961
Stephen Gerald Breyer, 1964
David Hackett Souter, 1966
John Glover Roberts, Jr., Chief Justice, 1979
Elena Kagan, 1986
Neil M. Gorsuch, 1991

In addition, there were such Harvard notables as presidents—Theodore Roosevelt, Rutherford B. Hayes, John Adams, John Quincy Adams, John Fitzgerald Kennedy, and hosts of other famous and successful graduates, including—Empress Masako, Empress of Japan; Birendra of Nepal, 11th King of Nepal;

Sebastian Pinera, President of Chile; Iván Duque, President of Colombia; Jacques Chirac, President of France; Shimon Perez, President of Israel; Pierre Trudeau, PM of Canada; Fan S. Noli, Prime Minister of Albania; Benazir Bhutto, First and Only Female Prime Minister of Pakistan; Tshering Tobgay, Prime Minister of Bhutan;

Robert Kennedy, Politician; Mark Zuckerberg, Businessman; Robert Frost, Poet and Writer; TS Eliot, Poet; J. Robert Oppenheimer, Scientist; Ralph Waldo Emerson, Academic; Henry Kissinger, Diplomat; W. E. B. Du Bois, Civil Rights Activist; Mitt Romney, Governor of Massachusetts; John Jacob Astor IV, Businessman; Leonard Bernstein, Conductor of New York Philharmonic Orchestra;

Isoroku Yamamoto, Japanese Naval Officer Who Conceived The Pearl Harbor Attack in 1941; Eugene O'Neill, Playwright; Gertrude Stein, American novelist; Michio Kaku; theoretical physicist, futurist; Cotton Mather, Church Minister; George Santayana, Philosopher, Essayist, Poet, & Novelist; J.P. Morgan, Jr., Banker; Henry Cabot Lodge, US Senator; Mike Pompeo, US Secretary of State; Felix Frankfurter, Judge; Aga Khan IV, Imam of Nizari Ismailism;

Adlai Stevenson II, Democrat Leader, Politician; Oliver Wendell Holmes, Sr., Physician, Writer; James Russell Lowell, Poet, Diplomat, Essayist, Writer, Literary critic, Journalist; Mario Capecchi, Molecular Geneticist,

Nobel Laurate; Learned Hand, United States Judge and Judicial Philosopher; Princess Carolina, Marchioness of Sala, Netherlands; C.I. Lewis, Philosopher;

and Joseph Pulitzer, Jr., Publisher, to add but a few distinguished names that the two young men could drop in careful conversations as they made their stepwise climb towards becoming interns and finally appointed justices of SCOTUS.

For Glen and Neal, the frosting on the cake of that first Monday in October and the first day of their first year as clerks for the famous new Chief Justice of the Supreme Court of the United States was to be formally invited to the white tie and tails gathering of the crème de la crème of Washington society at the ultra-exclusive Metropolitan Club on 1700 H Street NW. The soiree was also known as the annual Swine on the Vine charitable fund raiser, which was a golden opportunity to rub shoulders with almost everyone else who was one of the real Someones of the capital city.

Glen met two of the most conservative justices for the first time and had the rare opportunity to sit on a couch and discuss conservative politics. He was surprised to learn two things from Justice Clifton and Justice Rogers. He had no idea that the members of the Court were as blatantly political as they were in this cloistered and secure gathering, and he was further surprised that they would criticize the liberal justices as vehemently as they did the political ideology which drove their liberal colleagues.

Judge Rogers opened the conversation, "How was your first day, Glen? Did it measure up to everything you expected?"

"I was surprised, frankly, to see that the Chief Justice was so controlling and the associates so willing to comply with his demands, first of all, Your Honor."

"That will change soon. He is the new broom that sweeps clean; and I, for one, am glad to see the changes. But, once we get into serious debates on cases, you will see that you will have your work cut out for you."

"I'll bet. I presume the Chief's plan to increase the acceptance of the number of certiorari cases by a significant percentage will bring on more work for us lowly interns."

Judge Clifton joined in, "More work, I'm sure, but also more responsibility, more growth and development, and more risk of criticism. Comes with the territory. Your class of interns will likely be the most influential in the history of the Court, I would wager."

Neal entered the conversation cautiously, "But, Your Honor, won't most of what we do just become subsumed by the strong and differing opinions of our Justices; so, our input will be more voluminous, but less meaningful and influencing?"

"Only if you let it. Do good insightful work in succinct writing, and you will see your words and paragraphs eventually appearing in majority opinions, especially since you work for the Chief himself."

"I have talked to a few of his former interns in the Southern District and in Chicago. The consensus was that Chief Justice Cabot is a hard taskmaster, maybe more than a little intimidating."

"I heard the same, but I also heard that he is genuinely appreciative and rewarding of good work. I suggest you bone up thoroughly on his previous decisions and his law review writings. He is a stellar conservative thinker, this man to whom your futures are linked. Better get to know the man and his work if you want to survive and maybe even flourish, my young friend."

"Good advice, Your Honor, Glen and I have been doing that for the better part of a year; and we intend to keep doing the same thing for the next two years."

"A word to the wise. Check out what his confreres in CPAC are talking about, what the president is thinking, and what the base wants to hear. That will go a longways towards you getting the right stuff in your writings."

Judge Rogers glanced around the beautifully polished mahogany walls and immaculate tile floors with their hundred-year-old hand knotted carpets and spied some men with whom he needed to schmooze.

"Judge, I think it is time for us to have a few words with the Majority Leader and the John Birch people over there by the bar before they are unable to absorb our wisdom."

"Much as I am enjoying this conversation, Gentlemen, duty calls. We need to be sure our fellow conservatives don't feel left out. You know how it is."

The two justices left graciously and ambled over to enter the more important conversations going on among the movers and shakers.

The two interns could not help having a glint of stars in their eyes. This was their dream come true.

Five minutes later came the call, "Dinner is served."

Neal and Glen were famished after a very lean day, food wise. In fact, they had both skipped breakfast to be on time for meeting the Chief Justice; and he left them no time to have breakfast, brunch, or lunch. The tables were formal and set for a culinary educated clientele. Two plates, four spoons, four forks, two table knives and a serrated steak knife, two aperitif glasses, two wine goblets, and a crystal water glass.

"Which glass do you use for the Diet Coke?" Glen joked.

Neal shrugged and laughed.

"Good thing we had moms who cared about that kind of stuff," he said, "Can you imagine what this must be like for the interns from west of the Mississippi?"

"Both of them?" Glen answered, and they laughed again.

Actually, there were four: two from Arizona, and one each from Colorado and California, a matter of profound irrelevance to both Massachusetts interns. It would have been irrelevant even if they had bothered to find out somewhere during that hectic day.

Neal was seated to his right by Justice Isabela Duncan Parowan, arch-conservative, and renowned gourmand, and the Mayor of Cambridge, a middle-of-the-roader and renowned Italian lothario named Gaetano Saccomanno. He so looked the part that Neal had to suppress a little insider laugh.

It looked to be an interesting evening. Glen was assigned to a seat by Greta van der Brakel, a second-generation Dutch blond and intern for Judge Parowan, both of whom were somewhere to the right of Genghis Khan in their politics, a good mix for Glen. At least he could start off the year in comfortable company. On his other side, he sat by Jacques Baudelaire, an expat Frenchman who owned a very popular style salon in the city.

The meal was marvelous and lived up to all the folderal of so many knives, forks, spoons, dainty dishes, and glassware. Both young men settled on water and a red wine with a Frenchy name because they were going to have Beef Wellington and Veal Piccata respectively, and that way they were playing it safe.

For dessert, Glen had crème brulee which he loved, and Neal had two small Napoleons, because his father raved about the dessert so regularly that Neal thought it was about time he found out what all the fuss was about. It was marvelous, and he would be obliged to tell his father how much he had missed in his boyhood by being stubborn in his refusal to try it. He made a point to learn a bit about it to convince his father that he knew what he was talking about.

The French name, *Millefeuille*, means one thousand sheets which sandwich between their many layers a sweet almond paste, very similar to frangipane. The combination is the Napoleon. That he learned from *Ms.* van der Brakel, who made it clear that no one except her parents called her Greta.

After a polite period of after dinner pleasantries, the two young men gave each other silent signals that they needed to gain a little more information and experience than they could expect from the syrup and vinegar utterances that Ms. van der Brakel proferred.

"Let's get some air, Neal, and plan our next approach," Glen suggested, and Neal nodded his agreement with relief.

As the two very eligible bachelors leaned against the low brick wall separating the patio from the encroaching rose garden, Neal's suggestion for their next foray into the high society of Washington D.C. should be to find and get cozy with one of the liberal justices to gain a notion of how such ill-educated people in such influential positions thought about the current divisive political climate in the country.

Glen suggested that they track down Justice Mary Ruth Nichols who had been described as a "com-symp pinko" by each of their fathers when they were at their most generous in voicing their opinions of the liberal justices on the Supreme Court.

Neither young man took notice of a young couple dressed as upscale hippies—torn denims at the knees and mismatching long sleeve button dull-grey shirts–passed behind them. The male member of the couple began a violent coughing spell which caused Neal and Glen to turn around to see if the man needed help. Their last memory was of an intense cloud of white powder smoke blasting into their unsuspecting faces. The smoke cloud made them unable to cry out or to take a deep breath. In less than two seconds they were lying on the slate rock floor of the patio seeing the milky-way… then nothing.

CHAPTER

THREE

Chief of Capitol Police, Jake Hardman, was called away from his fine dinner of Peking Duck by a whisper from Det. Lt, 1, Harmon Frankfort Nivers. The two men left the dinner table with Hardman expressing his apologies.

"Sorry, Ladies and Gentleman, police duty calls."

Lt. of Detectives Nivers quickly escorted the chief out onto the rear patio of the spacious Metropolitan Club. Capitol police uniforms had closed off the crime scene with yellow tape and big bodies well before the lieutenant and chief arrived, and almost no one knew that anything serious had happened. Chief Hardman ordered his people to keep it that way until he ordered otherwise.

The medical examiner drew back the sheets covering the bodies; so, the two senior officers could get a close look.

"What's the powder on their faces, Doc?" Lt. Nivers asked as soon as the faces were visible and the most striking abnormality was apparent.

"Not sure yet, but probably some kind of poison, I would bet. I won't know for sure until we get them to autopsy and can get a couple of toxicity panels back."

"Any chance this is an infectious agent, Dr. Kindred?" Chief Hardman asked.

"Remotely possible, but I doubt it. The deaths were too quick. However, I am going to exercise a serious measure of caution and go ahead and get the hazards unit involved. They should be here anytime."

"The sight of the hazmat suits and their vehicles will freak out the crowd of swells. I'll have the building evacuated."

"How? or should I say where? are you going to interview them. These are hardly people who can be seen going into paddy wagons or into 119 D Street NE."

"Nobody's going to the Capitol Police HQ at this point, Doc. We'll take the rest of the night to interview everybody. And I mean everybody. I suspect my popularity rating will take a serious hit, but it has to be done. This is murder, and someone in this building this evening did it. I will know who when I'm done, or my name is not Jake Hardman."

"This is a 'tread lightly' case if ever I saw one, Chief. For all of us. I hate these sensational cases. Nobody wins. Are you going to get the DC policed involved, Jake?"

"Of course. It'll by CYA all the way. Lt. Nivers here will get hold of his nice friends at the FBI. You got it right, about this being sensitive and sensational. So, the more coppers we can get involved to spread the misery, the better, Doc. So, let's get to work and let the chips fall where they may."

After that conversation, it was all business. Dr. Kindred and his assistant opened the shirt studs of the two boys for a quick once over. There were no signs of foul play.

In a relatively unusual display of interservice cooperation, Capitol Police, DC Police, and the SAC of DC FBI agents and his elite interview unit spent the night grilling a large number of the highest-ranking officers of the several government agencies present as well as the cooks, custodians, janitors, administrators of the Metropolitan Club, and the crème de la crème of Washington's political scene. No one enjoyed the process. Names and threats were shouted at the cops, and they all—to a man or woman—behaved with admirable patience and courtesy while their ulcers had another workout. For all of that, the responses were "heard no evil, saw no evil, and no evil was spoken." For the forces of law enforcement, it was a complete bust.

Chief Justice Daniel George Cabot III gathered the other eight justices, all their interns, and every secretary, and told them about the "alleged" murders. His concluding remarks were a stern admonishment.

"Not a syllable of this reaches outside this group, understand? This sort of thing does not happen in our sort of people. Do not talk to the press, or to government officials. Refer everyone to the secretaries who will be deaf, dumb (in both senses of the word), blind, and retarded, and will refer any VIPIs to me where they will politely be told nothing but their own kind of political double-speak. We have to contain this, and we will."

Despite all the efforts to maintain secrecy, the *Washington Post* and the *New York Times* ran front page stories above the fold in their morning editions. The law enforcement chiefs and the justices swore that the leaker would be found and punished; but, as usual, they were all impotent in their efforts to find the culprit or culprits. That applied to the presumed murderers as well.

The quiet people went to work. The still warm bodies were delivered to 401 E Street SW, Washington, DC, the OCME [Office of the Chief Medical Examiner] bypassing any temporary BCP [Body Collection Point, with refrigeration]. Harold I. Kindred, MD, FACP, ASCP, FNAME, the chief, had received the bodies himself and met the investigators from the FBI, the Capitol Police, DCPD, and the White House.

"Gentlemen and Ladies, welcome to the preliminaries. Today, we will begin the three-part autopsy and forensic pathological examination of these two recently deceased individuals. I will be the lead in the forensic pathological portion of the investigation; and–by mutual agreement–the investigation in chief will be headed by FBI Senior Agent Mary-Margaret O'Leary from the Washington, D.C. Field Office, 601 4th Street NW, to clarify any question about whether the director and his office will be in direct control.

"I am going to start with fundamentals so that no one jumps to any conclusions. I am adamant about secrecy. No one and no organization will leak information. All communications with the press will be via Agent O'Leary and her office until the final forensic report is complete, then I will communicate that part of the overall investigation. Remember investigators, anything I tell you before that time is absolutely preliminary and may not be taken as anything but a part or a clue about where an investigation might lead.

"The crime scene investigation started last evening very shortly after these two bodies were found. So far, there is only one site of the crime scene; and that is the outdoor patio of the Metropolitan Club, located at 1700 H Sreet NW, Washington DC. Crime scene investigation is–by its most basic definition–the method of protecting, processing, and reconstruction, of a crime in every possible aspect. It doesn't matter where the crime took place or if there are more than one crime scenes involved; but so far we have only one place. We are fairly confident—although not absolutely certain–that the deaths of the two young men occurred at our crime scene and were not brought there from somewhere else.

"All crime scenes—and in this case the Metropolitan Club patio–are a source for physical and material evidence. However, the interpretation or reconstruction of a crime scene does not stop with obvious objects or clues. When investigating any crime scene, the investigator, whether police officer, detective or technician, must also take into consideration a philosophical approach to the scene. In this case, the political situation will have a role; but—here and now—I tell you that politics will not be the driving force any more than if this had been the murder of a cab driver in his taxicab.

"I admonish all of us as investigators as I have those at the crime scene that none of us should ever assume that we know what happened based on visual evidence alone, nor should we become biased or jump to conclusions when viewing any type of evidence, which includes physical evidence as well as witness statements. We will proceed with integrity and will reserve judgment until *all* evidence has been collected, analyzed, and then used to reconstruct this crime.

"We will have an orderly investigation and will proceed step by step until it is finished without allowing the press or other self-interested parties to obtain partial information. There are five major components to any Crime Scene Investigation process, and we will follow them:

"Teamwork: We have leadership, but no dictators. Everyone's opinion will be heard. We work together. I cannot emphasize that enough.

Documentation: No piece of evidence–however small or at first seemingly inconsequential–will be overlooked or neglected. All will be documented assiduously by the investigators.

Preservation: Always remembering that the vast majority of crime scenes are not permanent as such, two copies of documents will be kept. One by the investigator and held in readiness for use in later judicial actions and in the course of the investigation as needed. The other will be archived in my office—the OCME—and will be maintained as the complete record of the investigation, including objects that constitute actual evidence.

"Common sense will prevail even though we work in the greatest circus town on earth. We will speak to each other with comity and will listen with interest. From time to time, we will vote on the probative value of any piece of evidence to keep us moving forward. I will not tolerate brow beating or belittling to any degree. We will listen before we act.

"Flexibility: On that same note, we will all maintain an attitude that allows us to change our minds or to argue for evidence that we consider most probative. Do not fear having to change your stance when new or better information dictates. That is science; not believing, not religion. Nothing from on high at any level, even God, will sway us from our adherence to forensic science."

"The autopsy, or post-mortem examination which begins today will be conducted to help identify three elements of the crime: 1) the cause of death, 2) the mechanism of death and 3) the manner of death of the victims here in question. The investigation of any presumed crime—in this case alleged homicide—will be the purview of law enforcement investigators who will have full access to the autopsy evidence. What my people and I do here today will lead you to believe that this is a highly tedious activity. That is true.

"It is also exacting and important, too important to skimp or hurry through. Please follow me downstairs into the examination rooms. Let me remind you that there are refrigeration units all around, and the room is very cool–a word to the wise. Another one is, please have a strong person stand behind anyone who is new to this or thinks they might faint. We do not want any injuries among our investigators."

There were a few small nervous laughs.

Dr. Kindred led the assemblage to the stairs to the autopsy rooms proper—three flights down.

Everyone gathered around the first body, and the dinar removed the immaculate covering sheet exposing the corpse of Glen Lincoln Dastrup, so identified by his toe tag. A young capitol police officer fainted at the sight of his first dead body. His buddy behind him carried him to a couch along the wall, one of several provided for such occurrences.

"The autopsy begins with a careful inspection of the body," Dr. Kindred said into the morgue microphone, "and this is as far as we will get in this first session. Pay close attention."

CHAPTER
THREE

The greatest fear of everyone in the room—after that of fainting—was that of emitting a nervous titter, thus identifying himself or herself as a newbie, something akin to a grade-schooler.

Dr. Kindred talked as he deftly worked. The body had been in the morgue long enough to go into and then to release from rigor mortis and could be manipulated with relative ease.

"This first inspection can help establish identity, locate evidence, or suggest a cause of death."

The pathologists weighed and measured the body, noting the subject's clothing and valuables in the evidence bag. Dr. Kindred dictated his observations of the characteristics of "Mr." Dastrup's eye color, hair color and length, ethnicity, skin color, the lack of bruising or other signs of injury, the absence of tattoos, indications of skin disease or needle marks, sex, and apparent age.

"Note the purplish discoloration on his back skin. That is livor mortis, and merely indicates the settling by gravity as Mr. Dastrup's body occupied a supine position on his morgue slab until now. It is not indicative of trauma."

"What is the most obvious finding on this man in his current supine position, Agent O'Leary?"

"There is a copious amount of powdery substance around his face and neck."

"And it is quite obvious since it is rather thick," observed Dr. Kindred for the record. "Any thoughts, anyone?" The CME asked with the mike in the "off" position.\

"Poison," four of the investigators said at the same time.

"Weaponized anthrax."

"Tularemia, caused by Francisella tularensis; brucellosis, caused by Brucella suis; Q-fever, caused by Coxiella burnetii; botulism; Staphylococcal Enterotoxin B (SEB), toxin produced by Staphylococcus aureus, used as an incapacitating agent," said Ted Sorenson, from the DCPD.

Dr. Kindred laughed and said, "Nice try, Detective Sorenson. You can put away your iPhone for the time being. And, incidentally, I think the suggestions are all probably wrong including anthrax; death happened too fast. But, not to jump to conclusions, hold those thoughts."

Det. Sorenson blushed scarlet and sheepishly sneaked his incriminating smart phone into the pocket in the left side of his sport coat. He chuckled bravely at himself.

Dr. Kindred asked Drake Kinsey, the DCPD Chief of Detectives, to assist him and the young diener to move the young man's limbs, to hold them up for inspection, and to allow Dr. Kindred to move quickly with the joint mobility portion of the exam and to assist in turning him over into the prone position.

"We'll check very carefully for any obscured areas of trauma like abrasions or contusions hidden from obvious view in the areas of livor mortis. Mary Ruth, anything else I should pay particular attention to while Mr. Dastrup is in this uncomfortable position?"

"Yes, Sir. We should check for evidence of a stiletto or ice pick mark in the man's hair and for track marks in the posterior limb veins."

"Good. Here is a pearl. Very small pinprick marks can hide especially well in hairy areas or creases of the skin or in the skin of the buttocks. What is the importance of that, Dr. Nielson?" he asked the MD/PhD senior pathology resident, Alexander John Nielson, who was doing his Johns Hopkins Hospital rotation that semester and had just slipped unobtrusively into the rear ranks of the observers of the autopsy.

"How good of you to ask, Professor. I presume this is sort of a test since you pointed out just such a finding on a lawyer patient two weeks ago which proved to be the telling point in determining that the man had been murdered by a sneak attack injection poisoning with the hope that the person doing the autopsy would be too busy to turn the deceased over since, "nothing ever comes of it." Although the toxicology lab has yet to return their findings, it looks like we are going to be looking at another Georgi Markov type killing."

"You are such an overachiever, Doctor, Doctor Nielson. You have done so well so far, please continue to enlighten us ignorant Americans."

Dr. Nielson prefaced the rest of his communication with an appreciative laugh.

"All right, so we have the notorious case of the poison-tipped umbrella. Georgi Markov was a Bulgarian dissident newspaper reporter who rattled the cages of the deadly Bulgarian security agency. It was 1978 when Bulgaria and its secret service were puppets of the KGB of Russia. So, poor Mr. Markov reported feeling a prick on his thigh while standing on Waterloo Bridge in London. He died three days later. At autopsy he was found not to have any indication of natural causes of death. However, his astute medical examiner found a small wound on his thigh from which he extracted a 1.7 mm pellet which proved to be ricin, a very nasty poison—remember the Japanese subway mass murders.

"Then there was the eventually fatal poisoning of a former officer with the Russian spy agency FSB that sparked a major international incident. Litvinenko fell ill in November, 2006 after drinking a cup of tea laced with radioactive polonium. Investigators discovered that Litvinenko had met his killers in a ground-floor bar of the Millennium Hotel in Mayfair, central London. The investigators found that the pair were Andrei Lugovoi – a former KGB officer ostensibly turned businessman, who—after the deed–became a deputy in Russia's state Duma. His accomplice was one Dmitry Kovtun, a childhood friend of Lugovoi's from a Soviet military family. Vladimir Putin denied all involvement and refused to extradite either of the killers from Moscow.

ME Kindred added a case, "Perepilichnyy was a Russian businessman who collapsed while running near his home in Weybridge, Surrey in England in November, 2012, Alexander. His death was initially attributed to natural causes, but a pre-inquest hearing heard evidence from the autopsy toxicity lab search that traces of a chemical that can be found in the poisonous plant gelsemium were later found in his stomach.

The key finding by the investigators related to motive was that–before his untimely death–Perepilichnyy was helping a specialist investment firm uncover a $230 million Russian money-laundering operation. Hermitage Capital Management claimed that Perepilichnyy could have been deliberately killed for helping it uncover the scam involving Russian officials. A further pre-inquest hearing heard that he may have eaten a popular Russian dish containing the herb sorrel on the day of his death, which was the probable source of the poison.

Dr. Nielson continued, "In sum, the Russkies are bad actors who employ any means in their possession to do away with so called enemies of the state—read here, enemies of Putin or of the oligarchs. A Russian banker barely survived being shot four times by a silenced pistol. More than coincidentally, he had been involved in a bitter dispute with two former oligarchy business partners. It's not proof, but just sayin'."

"You ask the man for the time, and he tells you how to build a clock," Dr. Kindred said with an affectionate smile.

Doctor Doctor Nielson gave a small sweeping theatrical bow.

"So, my learned investigators, is this a variation of the Russian theme? Was it in fact, the Russians or their accomplices? Or copycats? Or home-grown haters who actually went to school and learned how to make poisons and such? And where do we go from here?"

Agent Mary Ruth O'Leary templed her long piano players fingers and thought for a moment before speaking.

"Is this the kind of thing our Russian friends know about? I mean, the powder substance that can kill someone in a matter of seconds, silently, and walk away before anyone is aware that anything is amiss? Are we focusing on the Russians when other bad actors are out there, like ISIS or the Taliban, or far-right wing American WASPS who went to the right schools and elected just to play dumb like the rest of the bubbas on the right? Or are we overlooking the BLMs, the Alt Righters, the Weather Underground, or Students for a Democratic Society?"

Dr. Kindred answered, "Any or all of them are suspects and should be investigated. But, we have to prove that it was murder first, then that the powder was the agent used. Be patient and don't jump on any particular band wagon just yet. There is a great deal we don't know, and we are likely to find more perplexing pieces of possible evidence before this is all over. I wish you success, my investigator friends. Since there is no such thing as luck, I will just have to note that this is going to be hard work, and I do wish you success. Keep in touch. You are all invited to the grand opening tomorrow. I am purposely holding up the intrusion in hopes that the lab findings will give us avenues to pursue."

CHAPTER
FOUR

With strong urging—to say the least—from the president, the chief justice, the director of the Federal Bureau of Investigation, the chief of Washington DC police, and four very conservative senators from the old Confederate South, the investigation into the deaths of Glen Lincoln Dastrup and Neal Crenshaw Gabler proceeded at breakneck speed even before the autopsy was complete.

Sybil Norcroft from the CIA used her wiles and her serious connections to get the movers and shakers from INTERPOL's chief, Kim Jong Lee, in India; the Russian FSB, CVR, and FSO; the Chinese, MSS and MPS; and even her inside spies in Iraq's RISF, and the internal security forces of ISIS; Pakistan's ISI, and the Pakistani political party JUI [*Jamiat-i-Ulama-i-Islam*]; and the Taliban's Ministry of Intelligence, and the Ministry for the Promotion of Virtue and Prevention of Vice, to have a look into possible suspects. She expended multiple markers to get that help.

In all, seventy-six special agents of the CIA traveled to forty-one countries in a secret whirlwind travel mission to ask the question, "Who was involved in the murder of the two US Supreme Court interns, why, and who were the leaders of the mission?"

One example will suffice since the brief interviews with foreign nationals and their intelligence and counter-intelligence services proceeded in much the same fashion. None of the US agents held any naïve opinions that the leaders of the groups they were to communicate with were any kind of bumpkins, ill-educated, inadequately trained, or inexperienced.

The experience of Lincoln Howard and Mac Young, the DCIA's go-to duo when something critical had to be done well, quickly, and quietly, was uniformly unproductive until they met external intelligence agents from the Taliban. The four men met in Asad Anwar Colony, Khyber Pahunkhwa Province, Pakistan. It was cold, and the perpetual wind blew a chill into the very bones of the men which served to move the pace of the conversation along more quickly. For the sake of convention, the men shared a steaming cup of fragrant chai but dispensed with the usual obligatory banal chat so favored by the Afghans.

"Tell us what it is you need to know, my *dostan* [friends]; and, perhaps, we can help you… for a consideration." Aakarama ibn Khan Zada Haji said.

"Of course, Aakarama, we would have nothing else. We are seeking the murderer of two boys who worked for our judicial system. We wonder if you have heard of such a crime or have knowledge of such a criminal? We are well aware of the astuteness of your intelligence services and the remarkable accumulation of detail as well as your command of current ongoing events."

Mac thought that Lincoln was plastering on the excessive bouquets even more than the usual requirements for dealing with Islamic war lords.

"We appreciate your language of respect, Shaqiq; and with time, we may be able to help. I shall inquire of the Deputy Heads of the Supreme Council. It may take some time," Aakarama said with somewhat less than enthusiasm.

"With respect, Brother, our esteemed leader DCIA Norcroft, has spoken at length with three of your most trusted leaders of the Supreme Council, namely, Tayyab Agha, Abdul Ghani Baradar, Shahabuddin Delawar, and Tayyab Agha, who have graciously offered any and all assistance we require in accordance with our growing agreement for the United States and its allies to leave your blessed country with dignity and to foster our growing friendship. Tayyab Agha, himself, was respectful enough to compose a letter in his own hand to be shown to freedom fighters such as yourselves. Your most capable leader Abdul Haq Wasiq also signed the directive. Would you like to see it, my Brother-in-arms?"

This was the make-or-break moment, and the tension began to rise. The two Afghan combat veterans reflexively began to caress the hilts of their curved *pesh-kabz* knives which were nearly ubiquitous among Afghan men as a personal weapon as well as a ceremonial badge of adulthood for Pashtun and other Afghan hill tribes.

Lincoln reached out the rolled parchment scroll—which was printed in handsome calligraphic Arabic and Pastun—to the pair of now less than affable tribesmen. For them to refuse would be tantamount to an intentional insult, and Lincoln and Mac held their breaths as the waited for one or the other of the sun, wind, and battle worn, fighters to make the first move.

Mohammed Nooruddin Raqib—who, to this point, had merely stood quietly behind Aakarama—molded his face into a definite provocative scowl and reached forward with his left hand to receive the missive.

Neither American made a move. The intended insult was too broad and deep to accept by any man.

Aakarama tapped Mohammed's arm and shook his head. Mohammed reluctantly switched hands to his right and accepted the letter. The Americans and Aakarama all took a breath. Aakarama quickly read the letter in both languages.

"We have learned of the man of whom you speak, but we cannot verify for certain that he is the perpetrator of the crime in your country. Here is a drawing of his face provided one of our tribesmen, and a short presentation of all we know of him as provided by the illustrious leader, Abdul Haq Wasiq, who is never the father of lies."

The Americans glanced at the drawing which was of a Han Chinese man in the heavy traditional clothing of an Afghan tribal fighter. The accompanying information indicated only that he was a traveling trader from Northern China, near the border with Vladivostok.

Aakarama ibn Khan Zada Haji said, "We hope this contributes to our growing brotherhood, my friends."

He smiled like a crocodile—all teeth and dead eyes.

The two American agents agreed, but only between themselves did they say, "Utter and useless BS."

Sybil Norcroft was grim faced when she gave the information gleaned from an expensive and time-consuming whirlwind of investigations around the globe.

"Special Agent O'Leary, here is my report turned over to you–essentially raw data. I'll save you time by telling you that we interviewed 1435 individuals in forty-one countries and came up with nada. Zip, zero, nothing. We even talked to the Taliban and might as well have been speaking Swahili to a pig for all the good it did us. Their leadership treated the news and the request for information as a joke and an opportunity to disrespect my best agents. No surprise there. Just off-hand, I think they are up to something big, and they are holding the information very close to their Shalwar Kameez coats [Afghan men's vests]."

"Thanks for the try, Sybil," Mary said. "I have something of a lead down in South Carolina which will require a very tough and sanguine lawman to get anything. Wish us luck.":

"I do," Sybil said with small shake of her blond tresses.

CHAPTER
FIVE

Major Jacklin Dobbs Henry of the Texas Ranger [known by many as *Los Diablos Tejanos* or TxDPS] Division Texas, was probably the only law enforcement officer—federal, state, county, or local—for whom the Alt-Right had any respect. Thrice he had risen to the rank of assistant chief, and he thrice had been demoted back to his present rank of major due to certain incidents resulting in grievous physical harm to men Maj. Henry insisted were participating in acts not permitted against women or children, for making the mistake of reaching for a knife during a gun fight, and for insubordination.

He stood six foot six, weighed 382 pounds, averaged a BP of 128/82, PR 52-61 (with exertion), had a BMI of 23, GFR of 96%, A_1C of 5.2%, LDL of 70, 20/15 visual acuity without corrective lenses, had never had an elective operation or hospitalization except for wound treatment, took no medications, refused vaccinations, and still retained his 32 adult teeth, which could not be said for many of the challengers he met from time to time while carrying out his ranger duties.

Maj. Henry was a confirmed retro in attitude, world view, courtly treatment of women, and fondness for children, dress, diet, and in response to political correctness. Rangers do not have a prescribed uniform, but most wear western clothing, hats, and boots. The major was easily recognizable for his mode of dress reminiscent of the old vaqueros: worn, but usually clean, denim shirts and pants; no tie, but sometimes a bandana around his neck; his saddle tac, spurs, ropes, and vests, were all fashioned after those of the *vaqueros.*

He mostly wore wide brimmed sombreros instead of cowboy hats, and square-cut, knee-high, high-heeled, and pointed-toe boots instead of modern low-heel, rubber-sole, round-toe, cowboy boots which were favored by most other Rangers. Like his fellow Rangers, Maj. Henry carried his hand-gun with the holster(s) positioned high around his hips instead of low on the thigh—this placement making it easier to draw while riding a horse.

He carried little ornamentation—his badge, a star cut from a Mexican silver five-peso coin which called to mind the Texas Lone Star flag. His only nod to modernity in dress was to accept the generally familiar "star in a wheel" style badge. On his ammunition belt, he had eight carved silver conchos and a silver and gold buckle. On the flap of his shirt, he wore the only medal he ever earned—the Ranger Medal of Honor, of which he was one of only twenty-one recipients since 1823. Like the vaqueros, Henry wore long spined Mexican Espuelas Charras spurs which jangled in a way irresistible to women of all ages as he walked into a room.

Jacklin (JD) Henry could be said to be ruggedly handsome with sun and wind etched topography, a strong nose, high cheekbones—a lean protector's face or the face of an unstoppable force, if you crossed the man. His teeth were large, white, and straight—better than most of his fellow Texans and the Rangers. He had a carefully trimmed and waxed long winged salt-and-pepper mustachio, and a neatly carved beard which pointed out from his cleft chin half an inch. His Adam's Apple was large and lean, and it served as a tell when he gambled or was about to shoot a bandito.

FBI Senior Agent Mary-Margaret O'Leary called Max Brandeis, Chief of the Texas Rangers three days after the SCOTUS interns murders on a conference call with David J. Griffen, Attorney General of Texas, and Carter Wilson Coppin, US Attorney General.

"Hello, Max, we have a problem you might be able to help us solve."

"No, 'how's the wife and kids or how about them Cowboys', huh? Let me guess; this has to do with the killings of those two young Supreme Court interns, and there's no time to waste,'" he answered.

"Dead on, Max. We need you to order your Jacklin Henry to get to the heads of the militias in the old Confederate South, Michigan, and northern Idaho and find out what they know. We need a name, and we need it PDQ… please."

"Glad to of service Mary-Margaret, but you need to know that nobody orders JD Henry around. I will "solicit" his help in a matter of national security importance. He knows everybody who knows anybody in the Alt-Right; and, if anyone can get information, he can. We don't question his methods, either. It's like having a mean old horse that can't be handled and asking the guy who takes care of such horses to do so. He always says he'll do it, but you don't get to ask him what happens."

"I'm aware of some of the major's exploits; so, do it your way. I just want you to be aware that POTUS and the Chief Justice are seriously interested. It can't hurt one's career to be seen as the one doing the helping."

"Gotcha, I'll get right on it."

On the fifth day after the murders, the toxicology report was received by Harold I. Kindred, MD at 401 E Street SW, Washington, DC, the OCME. He read it through carefully twice then put in a call to Special Agent O'Leary.

"Special Agent O'Leary, I pulled hard on some important strings and did some name dropping to get the tox report back in record time. This is explosive stuff. In brief, what they found was the powder on the interns' faces was weaponized radioactive polonium in an ingenious combination with strychnine—to make it extremely quick—and ricin. Nobody knew that those chemical formulae could be successfully mixed, or powdered, or delivered as an aerosol. We learn something new every day, I guess. Suffice it to say, the best minds in the toxicology world are working on all of those questions."

"Was this some sort of mad scientist who hates right wingers? Or some super rich BLM offshoot seeking revenge or power? Or… what?"

"I am not one to jump to conclusions, as you know, Special Agent, but maybe we should all be directing our attention to state actors."

"As if this was not difficult enough. Now we might be looking at an act of war… maybe by the Russkies, or the PRC. I can't even imagine an elite university lab acting on its own because the liberals in it want to wreck the recent right turn made by the Supreme Court as it is."

"I suggest that we all consider every imaginable possibility and also the unimaginable—leave no turn unstoned, as we say here in the national lab. You, Special Agent O'Leary, have really stepped in it this time and certainly have your work cut out for you. You might even think of getting the intelligence and national security people involved. As I recall, Sybil Norcroft over at Langley has a good nose for this kind of cloak and dagger stuff. Get her on the team."

"Good suggestion, Dr. Kindred, but Dr. Norcroft is already fully involved," SA O'Leary said.

CHAPTER
SIX

E vents overtook all the best laid plans of mice, men, and the FBI. Before the regular ideas could even be started towards their intended conclusions, the Supreme Court was to present an addition to the conundrum.

Greta van der Brakel, age twenty-six, was blessed at birth with pretty much everything a female needed to succeed; and she took advantage of every asset. She was lithe, healthy, energetic, white, bright, beautiful, had goodly and also wealthy parents with what amounted to a DAR list of personal connections that linked them with generational blue bloods dating back beyond the American Revolution when New York was still the New Netherlands. The family regularly dined with the likes of the Roosevelts, the Knickerbockers, the Onderdonks, and genuine descendants of Peter Minuit, Cryn Frederickz van Lobbrecht, Jan van Bonne, Willem Verhulst, Piet Johannes Megapolensis—who descended from a long line of Dutch pastors, all of whom originated with great, great... great grandfather Johannes; and Sophie van Doornmalen, senior cultural officer at the Dutch Consulate in Manhattan.

Greta and her family shared a tongue twister name of a nursery rhyme among themselves and with their upper echelon friends—the movers and shakers of New York and of the traditional conservative movement: *Trip a Trop a Tronjes* [The Father's Knee is a Throne]. They spoke old Amerikaans at gatherings for the fun of it. The family–and especially Greta–were very hard workers, and stinginess was hard-wired into their DNA. They took pride in the old dating style, "to go Dutch" especially when it was used along with the phrase "pinch-pennys" to describe their business spending methods.

Unlike her rather stodgy parents who were hidebound to tradition with girls and women being premier bakers, growers of prize roses, and *huisvrouws*, Greta chose to follow the law. She could have gone anywhere to law school, but she chose Harvard from which she graduated with highest honors and as the editor of the student *Law Review*. She was hired by the Wall Street accounting and law firm KPMG [KPMG International Limited–*Klynveld Peat Marwick Goerdeler*–an Anglo-Dutch multinational professional services network, and one of the Big Four.] It was a great plum for Greta Van Brakel, the brilliant and beautiful Dutch legal genius. The company was headquartered in Amstelveen, Netherlands, after incorporation in the United Kingdom. KPMG was a network of firms in 147 countries with strong Dutch influence—with Greta's Dutch connections helping materially in the application process.

Rather than take a major promotion within the firm, Greta used her accumulated good will and invaluable recommendations to gain the first of her two brief internships from among the 94 federal district courts: the Southern District of Alabama under Judge Kristi DuBose and the Eastern District of North Carolina under Richard E. Myers II, both conservative jurists of high acclaim.

Under their example and tutelage, Greta became well acquainted with Federal Questions related to: constitutional law, federal crimes, military law, intellectual property, securities law, and a few representative cases involving a law which the US Congress had passed. She was able to have her written work contained and credited in two of the cases passed on to SCOTUS.

Her application to receive an internship on the Supreme Court was hurried along by none other than famous conservative Justice Isabela Duncan Parowan. Nor was anyone particularly surprised when she landed the placement and was slated to serve her internship under that very same justice.

However, everyone who had ever heard of SCOTUS intern, Greta van der Brakel, was genuinely shocked, dismayed, and outraged, when on October 13th at 2204 hours she was shot in the head by a sniper who had been 800 yards away from her. The matter of her murder was very quickly reviewed by POTUS, the ODNI, and CIA headquarters, the NSA, the State Police of Maryland where the shooting took place, and the FBI.

The angry president, Irving David Duke, sat on a dais with Chief Justice Cabot III, Associate Justice Isabela Duncan Parowan, the DNI, the majority leader of the Senate, Republican Morris Richards of Tennessee, Carter Wilson Coppin, US Attorney General, and the Director of the Federal Bureau of Investigation, Luther Baum from Georgia.

The president rose, his face flushed; and his fists clenched.

"This a moral, legal, political, and possibly international, outrage. It appears obvious to me and to the Republican base, that this is a giant Antifa organized effort to destabilize our precious United States of America, to murder patriots, to create havoc against our sacred Constitution, and to further the programs of the ultra-left to make us into a socialist or a commie country.

"My administration will not stand for it. I will today activate the National Guard units, FBI and other state, federal, county, and local, law enforcement, our intelligence assets, the State Department, and my own direct connections among the true patriots of the nation. Antifa has adopted what it calls, 'Why not resort to Nazi punching?; maybe it is finally time to do some Commie punching.

"We have survived worse threats from the pinkos, and we will make quick hash out to these would-be traitors and insurrectionists. What law says that the society has be overrun by wet-backs, BLMS, or disgusting half breeds."

There was an awkward hush and many side looks passing around the elite crowd. No one could think of a comment or could muster enough information or gumption to ask a question.

Finally, the chief justice stood to speak.

"Yes, Mr. Chief Justice?" the president said recognizing his appointee.

"Mr. President, I believe the institutions of law and order and the judicial system itself is under direct attack. While we investigate, arrest people, and detain others, we must remember the rules of law and must be careful to make strong cases, whomever appears to be responsible here."

President Duke had a sneer on his face, and he took no effort to hide it.

"Whomever? Appears to be? Careful not to do anything politically incorrect? Injure the feelings of our Democrat friends? What have we turned into? Are we sympathizers with the commies, with the rioters, with the anti-patriots? Everyone in this room knows who it is… it is the traitorous Antifa, and it is time to stamp them out like the cockroaches they are. That is exactly what is going to happen, starting today with a rapid-fire series of presidential orders which will send Antifa running for the hills or, better, for Russia or Beijing where they'll be welcomed with open arms!!"

At FBI headquarters, the original task force, headed by Special Agent Mary-Margaret O'Leary, sat down to digest the facts, the fancies, and the political bombast, which was gaining force like a tropical storm that was on its way to be a hurricane.

"Special Agent O'Leary," one of the more recent graduates from Quantico, asked, "are we going to get the bureau embroiled in a civil war or an attack on Russia or China or both?"

"Over my dead body, Agent Haroldson. We are going to do what we always do. We are going to seek the truth and nothing else. We will investigate every possible lead and see where they take us. Right now, the main emphasis seems to focus on left wingers who hate the people on the right. I have to say that it seems too pat. I have a guy who knows the Alt-Right people, and I am hoping he can give us some direction.

"In the meantime, let's get everyone we can into the central city ghettoes and try and find out what they think is going on. Maybe we can find a trail that leads toward some crazies from BLM, Black Bloc, Black Nationalists, or even from environmental and animal rights groups, such as the Earth Liberation Front and Animal Liberation Front, which have—to this point in time—only made small attacks with few human deaths."

Another agent raised his hand.

"Aren't we neglecting the Islamic terrorism groups like ISIS, the Taliban, AQI, and their ilk?"

"Not entirely. We will have a small coterie of agents have a look, but home-grown Salafi-jihadists still pose only a limited threat, so far as our data show. The larger task force has given us the responsibility to check out the left. It seems unlikely that Antifa—the only major left-leaning group–would change its MO to initiate clandestine murders. They like the spotlight too much. However, who knows in this very confusing age? We'll give 'em all a good look."

The same young agent–a woman from upstate New York––added, "There is some rather confusing data available, but the overall conclusion is obvious: of nearly 900 politically motivated attacks and plots in the United States since 1994, there has been only one attack by an anti-fascist that led to fatalities. More broadly, and where the confusion lies in the reportage of the database, there have been 21 victims killed in leftwing attacks since 2010, and 117 victims of rightwing attacks in that same period. That is awful even on the part of the left, but the white supremacists still account for almost six times as many deaths**.**"

"All true and duly noted. Believe me, I am tuned into the White Separatists, White Supremacists' station, and concomitant with our limited action in the beginning, they are well under our radar. Let it suffice that I have a guy."

Everyone laughed because Mary-Margaret O'Leary was famous for having a "guy" to handle just about any contingency.

Major Jacklin Dobbs Henry of the Texas Rangers responded to his chief, Max Brandeis's, call and request. Since whether to accept and how to proceed was left to his discretion, JD acquiesced with alacrity and a goodly measure of enthusiasm. He did some preliminary investigation to learn where his quarries were currently hiding out, then collected his horses and gear and set out on his solo ranger mission.

Maj. Henry elected to start in his home state of Texas with its 54 separate hate-group entities, all acting under the well-advertised White Supremacist rubric. Nor was it particularly difficult to gain access to the leaders and their compounds. Everyone had a well-marked, fortified, and guarded compound. Henry's notoriety had preceded him, and the entities were glad to have him come by as a diversion.

White Supremacist Terrorism is—for the most part—tedious work. Most of it consists of meetings to hear the same rhetoric coming from different men and women from units around the country, even the world, who were like thinkers. It is not just great minds that think the same way. Marching around in a heavy pack carrying heavy ordnance, running about and hiding in the same old places in the four-acre forested plots, and attending occasional disruption marches with minor clashes with Antifa groups, all got old over time. Having a genuine old-time American Texas Ranger come by was a novelty, and Henry collected a fairly large number of followers and admirers.

That was not useful for his investigation. Dallas, Houston, Austin, Granbury, Irvine, Kerrville, San Antonio, and Temple were busts—complete wastes of time–the militias there largely consisting of wannabe kluckers, anti-Muslim fighters, race baters, anti-semites, Neo-Nazis, and general haters in the name of Christ. None of them had seen action, even though many were former cops and soldiers.

The place in Texas that did provoke some interest on JD Henry's part was in the outskirts of DeKalb, Texas where the well-guarded, clean, and ominous, Church of the Ku Klux Klan seemed to prosper out beyond the suburbs. The Ku Klux Klan, with its long history of violence, is the oldest and most infamous of American hate groups. Although Black Americans have typically been the Klan's primary target, it also has attacked Jews, immigrants, members of the LGBTQ community and–until recently–Catholics.

A purge of VK (a Russian social media network popular with the Klan) earlier in the year severely limited the visibility of many Klansmen, while constant infighting and an inability to resolve conflict had the largest impact, making the Klan increasingly insular.

Few new members were being recruited to the remaining Klan organizations in general. But the Church organization in DeKalb seemed to be flourishing: new outbuildings, an addition to its hunting/training land plots, the best and latest ordnance by far–and best of all–a significant increase in fired up new recruits ready to save the white Christian race no matter what sacrifices had to be made by the mud-people, the ragheads, the wet-backs, or the Christ killers.

The Church of the Ku Klux Klan stood out to Major Henry and loomed as fertile ground for his investigation, and he made a beeline for the rural town of less than 2,000 people which seemed to be a good deal more prosperous, more active, more religious, and demographically younger, than any other Texas town of comparable size. Something was going on, and that something smelled of fish to the ranger.

Maj. Henry made a polite telephone call to the putative head of the KKK Church in DeKalb and was surprised and pleased to connect with the "pastor" directly and immediately.

"DeKalb Righteous Baptist Congregation. How may I help you, Sir?"

"Am I speaking to the pastor?"

"Indeed, I am privileged to be so titled. May I ask your need, Brother?"

"I am Major Jacklin Dobbs Henry of the Texas Ranger Division. What is your name, Brother?"

"I am Pastor Reggie Quarler Wells, and the Grand Wizard of the Klan in these parts. Your reputation and fame precedes you. Are you calling on police business, or are you thinking of becoming part of our movement to restore the rightful place of the white-skinned majority in this country of ours that seems to be losing its way?"

"Pastor Bradshaw, I am part of murder investigation, and we need your help to bring in the killer or killers to justice."

"Is it one of the Antifa hitmen?"

"Don't know yet. I would like to palaver with you to see if you know anything or anyone that might help the rangers with a lead. I'd like to do business with you mano-a-mano. I do better facing a man or men than I do with the electronic contraptions that keep popping up and complicating things. How are you fixed for time this afternoon, Pastor?"

"That'd be a good time, Sir. Come on over 'bout two, would that fit your schedule?"

"It would. I'll be there then."

"We have a comfortable barn and some cottages we keep for visitors. It requires an hour's horseback ride to get there. You okay with that?"

"Sure. I'll bring along my horse and trailer."

"*And three handguns, a long rifle, and a short-barreled shot gun,*" added Henry, but only in his mind.

CHAPTER
SEVEN

Since the "Intern Murders" task force [as dubbed by the media] lacked any other enforcement personnel who understood or spoke hillbilly or the way of thinking among the survivalists, or others making up the Alt-right, the force had to do its interviewing the hard way. Simultaneous no-knock raids were carried out on the seven main hate groups in Coeur D'Alene and Meridian, Idaho [Neo-Völkisch Asatru Folk Assembly, G415 Patriots, Independent History & Research general and Anti-Muslim haters], the Lordship Church in Bonner's Ferry, Soldiers of Odin, eight locations each statewide anti-Muslim hater units, Brother Nathaniel Foundation headquartered in Priest River, and Aryan Brotherhood and Patriot Front, loosely associated White Nationalist and anti-African-American groups throughout the state of Idaho.

DCIA Sybil Norcroft and President Duke separately, and at nearly the same time, suggested that the task force hire its own private investigation firm to handle the intelligence work necessary to ferret out the information about who was who, where, and when. Sybil had had numerous dealings with a firm called MacGee and Associates, and had always found them to be reliable, courageous, intrepid, and expensive, commensurate with the quality of their work.

She suggested MacGee to the president who brushed off the fact that MacGee was expensive—since he, the president, was using OPM–other-peoples'-money–suggested the idea and the one firm to SA O'Leary. The putative advantage as seen by the task force was the fact that new and civilian faces would be less memorable, and less antagonistic, seeming than the unmistakable look of FBI faces.

Sybil said, "Not to horn in, but it might be better if I called MacGee on his private line since he and I know each other, and it will be more efficient. You and I are both busy, but—at the moment—you are busier than I am, right?"

"Yes, Ma'am, I am busier than the proverbial long-tailed cat in a room full of rockers. It would be much appreciated if you would handle the private investigation entirely, including reportage. You can keep me and the president in the loop. If I understand President Duke correctly, MacGee gets to use a black credit card."

"Apparently. He won't abuse the privilege, I can tell you from ample past history with him and his two associates, Ivory White and Caitlin O'Brian, the firm is not exactly thrifty, but they are assiduously honest, and worth every penny they are paid and that they spend."

"Well," Mary-Margaret said, "I trust you; so, I guess I will just have to go ahead and trust them as well."

"Okay, I'll get right to it," Sybil said, "and I wish you success in dealing with our very 'special national base with God on their side exclusively'."

Ranger JD Henry's first observation as he drove into DeKalb was of a large billboard, and a small but professionally made sign on a private front lawn: the billboard read–"DeKalb White Unity Meet & Greet, "All White Christian Patriots are welcomed but must contact the Church of the Ku Klux Klan for further information to attend." And in small letters below, "Aryan Freedom Network."

On the private land, the sign said—"The Coalition of anti-racism groups has organized a demonstration against a planned Ku Klux Klan meeting in DeKalb, call 903-682-7087." That was countered by a plethora of recruitment flyers on telephone poles along neighborhood streets and on other back lawns. JD had a hot, dry, boring, hour-long, ride, from the hitching rail in front of the Ku Klux Klan Church in DeKalb city proper to the fine multi-gabled, highly varnished, and perfectly caulked, log house in the middle of nearly a dozen similar but much smaller, log cottages near the Arkansas border.

All the buildings–including obvious utility structures– had green aluminum rooves and red doors. Although there were no uniformed guards, and none stationed in front of any of the many doors, the presence of security was obvious to the trained eye of the ranger. In fact, he found the security personnel so easily, that he presumed it must have been intentional to create the feeling that this was a part of Texas not to mess with.

DeKalb is in Bowie County in the northeastern part of the state, part of the tripoint of borders–of Texas-Oklahoma-and-Arkansas. The county is mostly East Texas Timberlands set in loam or clay soil and nourished by frequent and more than adequate rainfall. The terrain is level or at most uneven; it is gently rolling and ranges in elevation 200-450 feet above sea level. The county is bounded on the north and south by the Red and Sulphur rivers. Bowie is excellent agricultural country.

The DeKalb Ku Klux Klan Church's [aka- DeKalb Righteous Baptist Congregation] pastoral residence is set off on a rutted dirt road in a part of the county and has a formal address that is merely a post office box number. The area is considered by many political right leaning people as a part of Arkansas and that it should be an all-white security zone.

As it is, the demographics revealed in decades of census taking as very stable at about 94,000 people, 60% white and 25% black of Bowie County overall, with a changing mixture in the remainder. The section of the county where the church and its pastoral residence is located and where there was rumored to be an historically important rally of the klans in a month is 98.6% white. Organizers hope for a certain famous billionaire who is a gifted motivational speaker to give the keynote address.

The KKK is the largest hate group in Texas, and its secret tentacles reach everywhere in the northeast Texas county.

Into this milieu, rode the Texas Ranger law enforcement ranger alone, the "one riot, one ranger" representative of official law and order. He hobbled his horse and left the handsome bay under the shade of a towering 90-foot-tall red oak tree, the only one in the county.

Knowing that multiple eyes were taking him in, JD brazened his way to the front door of the church making no attempt at stealth or being quiet about it. His silver spurs jangled conspicuously as he walked up the four wooden front steps and stopped in front of the heavy oak door of the official and very exclusive residence of the KKK clericals.

The door held a large sign reading: "White Democrats, Mud People, Jews, and Commies, stay locked up in your homes, the KKK is coming to DeKalb September the Eighth for the First Historical Rally since the illegal Washington cabal outlawed slavery and killed thousands of innocent "White American Patriots", the light-hearted notice said. Undaunted, he knocked three times with unabashed authority.

The door opened, and Pastor Reggie Quarler Wells of the KKK Church and Grand Cyclops of the congregation and its mixture of klansmen from the White Knights of Texas, Knights of the Red Hand, the Pale Faces, the White Brotherhood, the Constitutional Union Guards, and, in Texas only, the Knights of the Rising Sun, and the Knights of the White Camellia opened it.

"Ah, Ranger, welcome, welcome. Step into my parlor," the pastor said with a broad grin.

JD completed the pastor's sentence, "*said the spider to the fly*," but of course, only in his mind.

"Glad to be here; thanks for the invite on such short notice," he said.

"Always happy to accommodate the fine officers of the law," Pastor Wells said and extended his work calloused hand to the ranger.

"*Even though we don't recognize any such authority from the Washington 'replacers', 'libbers', 'cuckservatives', 'elites', and 'racial-guiltists'.*" He said mockingly again in the recesses of his mind with a soda-cracker expression still on his face.

"Y'all requested a palaver," Wells said, "but y'all wasn't too specific. What do you want from us Patriots?"

"How about a chair to take the weight off my achin' back for starters," JD said with his most friendly face.

"Sorry… I am forgettin' my manners. My mama taught me better."

He led the way to a comfortable set of armchairs in the back of the reception area.

"Thank ya kindly," JD said.

"Can I offer y'all somethin' to wet yer whistle?"

"I'd like that."

"Y'all look like a bourbon and branch water sort of man, am I right?"

"That'd be fine. Okay if you make it a double?"

"Comin' right up."

He raised his right index finger and a waiter wearing a long sleeved white klan shirt stepped into the room.

"Coupla full glasses, Ned, if y'all wouldn't mind. BB&W."

Ned exited and returned in a minute with large mugs full of amber liquid with a twig of a fresh young Douglass fir tree floating in it.

JD let the 'Grand Cyclops' talk as they sipped their drinks. He recited an all-too-familiar litany of White Supremacist, populist themes: "closed borders," anti-racist Guilt," " reinstatin' Western chauvinism" "reinstatin' slavery in select correct thinkin' states, America for the White Race, anti-Semitism, anti-Muslim, anti-abortion for white women, "proper masculinity," "savin' Confederate flags and statues," and "getting' ridda the State Department and its foreign giveaways."

The ranger thought his eyes would glaze over if the soliloquy lasted much longer. He had heard it all before and did not necessarily disagree with the majority of the opinions. But he had come to do a job.

CHAPTER

EIGHT

Special Agent Mary-Margaret O'Leary and her select task force—now including Ivory White from MacGee and Associates—moved into the Bedford Stuyvesant neighborhood as unobtrusively as possible and began to seek out gangstas they could talk to. They came armed with a list of NYPD's CI list for the area as a useful leg up. The nearly coal black skin color of Ivory and one of the regular FBI special agents, Dikembe Anderson, was worth more than just a leg up. It made all the difference.

The two men ceased shaving, combing their hair, brushing their teeth, or bathing for three full days. They searched online and bought very cheap, poorly made FuZhiBang NYU14 "The New Crocodile" gold alloy baseball caps that all but glowed in the dark, plain grey hoodies, beanies, skull caps, tall sneakers, heavy fake gold chains and large "gangsta" rings that could serve as brass knuckles. They placed the clothes in dirt piles at the dump and walked on them for ten minutes to give them the desired cache.

Experts applied fake tattoos to serve as the tattoo arm sleeves so incredibly popular at the time in the 'hood. They were pleased that the result was entirely characteristic of prison tats… and that they would reliably wear off with time. Neither man would have agreed to have a real tattoo, even after being dead. When they were satisfied that they were fully ripe, and that they looked and dressed the part, Ivory and Dikembe set out to procure a ghetto ride: a 2010 Toyota Highlander hatch back, not gently used which ran well despite its mournful looks occasioned by two motor vehicle accidents minus repairs to the plastic body.

Then the two erstwhile wannabe gangstas moved into an apartment on Tomkins Avenue, Brooklyn less than two blocks from the 79th Precinct located at 263 Tompkins Avenue, a crowded and overly busy street that no one could argue its slum bona vides.

No one brought cookies, of course, but Ivory and Dikembe were cordially invited to become part of their new neighborhood's robust economic atmosphere. Three days after arrival—presumably as ex-cons recently released from Rikers—both men were the recipients of invitations to join the Hoolies, the Humble 800s, the 900s, and even by a small remnant of the Crips. They played coy for a day or two; but the Hoolies made an offer they could not refuse; and the pay was the best of all the tempting offers; so, the two men became enthusiastic Hoolies.

Their first job was to rob the Pep Boys store on 354 4th Ave, a store that had been robbed three times a year for a decade. It was to be a B&E rather that a brazen mid-day armed robbery complete with pyrotechnics, broken doors and windows, wounded and dead bystanders, and cops, especially lots of cops. They were to smash and grab the cash from the till and as many boxes of lithium batteries as they could carry. It was presumably a test, but the crime involved was a felony. Ivory and Dikembe both expressed concerns about the possibility of a mishap and having a civilian be shot.

Ivory had the simplest and least worrisome solution.

"We'll call the task force and get them to bring the Pep Boys' merchandise to us two undercover agents, and we take it to the gang and get kudos or gold stars stuck to our foreheads, however they handle such things."

"We can try," Dikembe said.

The two men went out to dinner at the Crab House Buffet at 135 E 55th Street, in Manhattan, well away from the grubby likes of their newly adopted gang. After the sumptuous meal beginning with fresh raw blue point oysters and steamed clams as appetizers, followed by courses of salt and pepper Dungeness crab, fresh live lobster, with Cajun drawn butter, and jumbo crab legs with old bay dipping sauce. The side dishes were fresh corn on the cob, coleslaw, mixed green salad, and boiled red potatoes. They drank a whole bottle of excellent Chablis. The government paid for their indulgence with its famous black credit card.

As Ivory and Dikembe enjoyed their working meal, the other members of the task force gathered up Pet Boys trademarked goods and dumped them into a dirty blue nylon laundry bag for authenticity. The gang swallowed the ruse hook, line, and sinker. The two newbies were in.

The gang members loved to drink and were not picky as long as it was alcoholic. When pleasantly liquored up, they shared the gang's secrets freely with their new buddies. What they did not do was even to suggest that they knew anything about the murders of the two SCOTUS interns, let alone who did the deed. Their friends were also totally nonplussed when asked about the murders or any possible murderers. Ivory and Dikembe had come to a complete blank despite all their hard work and great danger–situations the two men had a good laugh about.

"What do you think about our informants, Ivory?" Dikembe asked as they signed their mission reports.

"There are a few villages around missing their idiots," Ivory said, and that was that.

Special Agent Randolph Peterson was still easily identifiable for his negroid facial characteristics despite his light café a lait complexion. As his part of the task force to ferret out the killer of the two SCOTUS interns, he volunteered to meet with the leader of the BLM [Black Lives Matter] movement, Dewan Trebelle.

Peterson prided himself for being a patient man; he handled long boring stakeouts with relative equanimity— better than his fellow agents—but after hanging around the gangsta's smoke filled apartment and having to sit on a couch that he suspected had some crawlephants in it, he was getting antsy.

"Hey, you guys," he said, "I've been pretty patient here, but I've got other work to do. When's you man, Trebelle, gonna show?"

"He'll be here. It ain't great for the rep to have a fibbie hangin' in our crib all day; ya get my meanin'?"

"Of course I do, and I'll be outta here a few minutes after the man shows. Try pingin' his cell again, okay?"

The man he knew as Devil's Friend, groused about it; but he called one more time. No luck. The two BLM leader's junior officers assured SA Peterson one more time that Trabelle would be along any moment.

However, Peterson's intel was better than they suspected. The FBI IB had found out that Trebelle was currently hallucinating and being held in a padded room donated by a BLM contributor for his own protection. The chief intelligence agent on the case explained:

"Trabelle has a habit of trying pretty much any new drug or fad in drug use that he got wind of. Near as we can tell, he seems to have gotten hold of some variant of the Angel's Trumpet flower. He fell in love with the euphoria and hallucinogenic affects of AT and could not back away from repeated use. His subordinates told me that he has had a pharmacist mix, mingle, and integrate different types of AT flowers, their stems, and leaves.

He finally succeeded in producing very long acting and considerably more potent hallucinogens than were previously known. He has been out of this world for over a week with no signs of the effects diminishing. Thus far, the subordinates have been able to keep this information away from the rank and file and from the Alt-Right who would have a field day with it, but it doesn't look like you are going to get anywhere anytime soon. Sorry."

"I have interviewed a dozen or more people who have been active in the marches, the looting, and in defending the anti-conservative agitators. None of them know anything about any assassins, killings, vendettas against SCOTUS, or anyone else. We have drawn a blank with the BLM. Trebelle is the last man I have to question, and none of us have any idea when he will be able."

"So, your report will have a hole in it… happens to the best of us, Agent Peterson. I will keep an eye on him; and, if he comes back from la la land sometime, you will be the first one I tell about it. Maybe you can salvage something then. Have any of the agents found a useful lead?"

"Not that I know about."

Agent Peterson spent the rest of the next ten days moving from New York to Chicago to Omaha to Houston and finally to Brooklyn Heights in Los Angeles to meet with the other branches of the BLM and lesser organizations in the radical sphere like the NAACP, the CRC [Civil Rights Congress], the WeChargeGenocide movement, and the NCNW [National Council of Negro Women].

After an exhausting hectic week of travel and seemingly endless talk, SA Peterson decided and said so in his formal report that the organizations of Black activism were—on the whole—quite tame and no threat to the stability and well-being of the United States. Most importantly, for the purposes of the investigation, Peterson was convinced that the African-American politicians in general knew nothing and had done nothing of note to further the assassinations of the SCOTUS clerks.

Partners Miguel Asai Montego [Latino] and Beshiltheeni Begay [Native American] were appointed to investigate the reservations and larger general communities where Latinos and indigenous Americans lived—Santa Fe, Los Angeles, Anchorage, Oklahoma City, Phoenix, and New York. The work had been made much easier because of the general cooperation by the ethnic groups represented in these categories. The two agents were able to make swift progress by meeting with large groups in theaters and sports facilities.

Their facility with the minority leaders and their languages was of inestimable value. Not a single person had anything to contribute. Montego and Begay were convinced that they were getting the truth, and that there was no conspiracy, guilty knowledge, or involvement, by anyone. They left for DC disappointed that they had not been the agents to break the case but heartened by the conviction that none of their families or friends had done anything to bring down shame on their people.

CHAPTER
NINE

Texas Ranger Henry listened to Pastor/Grand Cyclops Wells drone on about his saintly life as a Christian advocate for the oppressed white people for nearly two hours. But he drew the line when Wells began to stray off into anti-vaxxer, border security, votes stolen by progressive crooks in the electoral process, and how the good people of Texas had been robbed by "The Lefty Leaning Supremes by their "pro-abortion rulings."

"Hey, Reggie, I appreciate y'all's openness about your group's opinions and how much you personally are doin' to further the cause of White People; but I ain't got all day, ya know. I need y'all ta focus on the crime I'm investigatin'. Tell me anythin' and everythin' y'all know about them eastern boys who got themselves kilt. See or hear anythin'? Got any serious suspicions? Any a your boys make a comment that might put me on the right track?"

"Much as I would like to help, ya kin count on that; but I haven't a clue. Ain't heard nothin', seen nothin', or learnt about nothin', that'd help. We don't do no assassinations, and we don't know anybuddy who does. Cross mah heart, Ranger."

"Then, I better be on my way, Reggie. I'll take ya at your word, but I sure don't want ta find out that you were… mistaken, if ya get my drift. It wouldn't go good for none a y'all."

"Ah swear on my oath as a Klansman that I don't know nothin'."

Henry eased his lanky self out of the comfortable chair.

"Thanks for the hospitality, Reggie. Keep yer nose clean and don't git inta any trouble, now, ya heah."

He said it with a smile, and the two men shook hands. While Henry did not exactly admire the Kluckers, his gut told him that this one was telling the truth, and he said so in his report.

It fell to Agent Sam Overly, Jr. to head up the investigation dealing with the many US religions to find out what the leaders and the rank-and-file knew or even suspected. He and his partner knew it was an impossible task to be really thorough, but they were going to give it a serious try.

They enlisted help from cops of all stripes all over the fifty states. Overly insisted that the best way to get information was to go softly, no "good cop, bad cop" routine. He saw to it that cops of the same religious persuasion talked with the disparate religious people: Mormons to Mormons, Catholics to Catholics, Born Agains to Born Agains, and what Overly called Wild Honyocks to Wild Honyocks, etc. They were not to be accusatory, demeaning of doctrine they did not understand or disagreed with, nor to argue over anything.

Like many FBI agents, Overly was a member of the Church of Jesus Christ of Latter-Day Saints—a title they much preferred over "Mormon"; so, he assigned himself to interview the presidency and the Twelve Apostles—total fifteen. He had to do it one man at a time and strongly admonished the interviewees not to divulge what his investigation was about until he had had a chance to talk to every man.

Agent Mickey O'Shaunessy had the daunting task of interviewing 221 cardinals and the 34 active Roman Catholic archbishops in the United States, of which five are also cardinals; so, there was some minor redundancy. For the purpose, he was given twelve full-fledged agents and an equal number of Quantico trainees to ease the load.

The task leader, Mary-Margaret O'Leary and six other agents took on the daunting job of meeting with the most far-right clerics in the country—an even one hundred of them–who were expected to be resentful and closed-mouthed. She asked MacGee and his two associates, Caitlin O'Brian and Ivory White, to help, once Ivory got done pretending to be a gangsta.

Agent Abu Bakr al Mecca–born Steve Donovan–before his conversion, took charge of interviewing the prickly Sunni imams and Shia Twelvers and imams—a very small number.

Two examples should suffice:

Interview of Jack Isaiah Brown, Pastor of the Church of the Faithful Born Agains in Jackson, Mississippi by Special Agent Mary-Margaret O'Leary.

O'Leary (O'L)—Thank you for taking time to meet with me, Pastor Brown. I know you are very busy; so, I will get right to the point. You have no doubt learned something about the murder of two young men and a young woman who were Supreme Court clerks. I need your help in trying to find who did these terrible crimes.

Brown (B)—As if I had any choice. The federal government that I don't even recognize, demands it, and so, here I am. Every time some n—- gets killed—and usually by someone from BLM, I get a visit. Same with anyone from the government gets murdered when he or she pokes their nose into where it doesn't belong. So, ask your invasive and impertinent questions and get this interrogation over with.

O'L—Just for clarity, Pastor. These were very strong conservative whites.

B—Whatever.

O'L—I and the United States government need to know who killed these people and why. Please take the time to give me an honest answer.

B—I don't give a fig about you, your terrorist organization, or your illegal government, but I always answer honestly. I am ordained minister of God, in case you are unawares. I don't know anything more than I read in the "Fake News", and that doesn't amount to a hill of beans. I have not heard of anyone in or out of the true Christian world who would do such a thing, nor have I seen anyone who acts or speaks suspiciously. And incidentally, I always speak the truth. Period. Anything more I can do for you, Msss. Agent?

O'L—No knowledge of clandestine meetings, any of your parishioners made odd seeming trips to DC lately, that sort of thing?

B—Stolid silence.

Interview of Imam Haji Ahmed bin Abdullah, leader of the Michigan Islamic Studies Center, Detroit, Michigan.

O'L—Thank you for your taking time to meet with me and for your much appreciated cooperation. I presume you are aware of the three murders of Supreme Court Interns in Washington DC recently, and I am here to enlist your help in my investigation.

IH—We proud Americans seek Allah's help to keep us on the straight and narrow line with the laws of our United States. What is it you wish to know from me exactly, kind sir?

O'L—Do you have knowledge from your acquaintances, your family, or your congregation about those murders? Someone boasting? Someone praising Allah that the Supreme Court has been punished, anything like that?

IH—I have not. We pay very little attention to your judicial system. We have our own, and most of our conversations about law center around what the imams are saying and doing within God's laws—the Sharia.

O'L—Are you aware, Imam, of any of your youth going astray and being recruited by terrorist groups, any young people whose parents have expressed concern.

IH–No, *alhamd lilah*, we have thus far been spared such sin. No one from our mosque has ever fallen into such disgrace.

O'L—Yes, praise God.

The task force investigated the LDS church, the Jehovah's Witnesses, and sent e-mail inquiries to the mainstream Protestant churches and smaller Catholic and Orthodox communities. The results of that effort were the same as for all the religious, criminal, law enforcement, and those interviewed by Maj. Henry of the Texas Rangers. They were probing a dry well with a forked stick in a desert.

CHAPTER

TEN

It was a bad day for Special Agent Mary-Margaret O'Leary when the final reports came into the task force center from all the agents, law enforcement officers, and the MaGee Investigations firm. No one anywhere had seen anything, heard anything, suspected anything, produced any useful data, eyewitnesses, or even crazies who confess to any new murders. Apparently, the latter were busy with other delusions. The news was not just all bad, but SA O'Leary had to convey it all up and down the line: to DFBI, DOJ, DCIA, Office of the President, the ODNI, Chiefs of Police throughout the country, and worst of all to the boiling mad parents of Glen Lincoln Dastrup, Neal Crenshaw Gabler, and Greta van der Brakel, all of whom wanted her head on a pike.

SA O'Leary wanted to cry or to tear out her hair, to scream on the top floor of the FBI Building in Washington DC, or to cut her wrists. She did none of that. Instead, she sucked it up like good FBI agents do and began thinking hard about a next step if she were to be allowed to keep her position in the task force.

Mary-Margaret was humble enough to seek advice from people she truly trusted which included DFBI Owen Murdoch and Sybil Norcroft at the CIA who had been known to pull a rabbit out of a hat in the nick of time more than once.

Sybil asked Mary-Margaret if she would mind including MacGee and his Associates and two of her most trusted agents, Lincoln Howard and Mac Young, who had been around to help pull the rabbits when the situation seemed to be impossible.

In the interest of maintaining absolute secrecy, the meeting was held in MacGee's secret hideaway in the Yellow Breeches Creek area of south-central Pennsylvania in Michaux State Forest, a great place to catch trout; it is famous for stocked brown trout, but few people visit there off season. In compliance with a presidential request forwarded through the head of Pennsylvania Fish and Wildlife, fishermen were told that the stream was closed for the week while Fish and Wildlife rangers investigated reports of possible infestation with schistosomiasis causing parasites.

Before the meet and greet pleasantries were over, SA O'Leary received a sat-phone call.

Only her half of the conversation could be heard, but that was enough:

"Hello."

"Yes, it is."

"Who? Say again, reception is imperfect."

"Where did it take place. Was the justice hit?"

"How bad?"

"Two of them, you say? Any witnesses? Is there a suspect?"

"How is that even possible?"

"Sorry, I meant no criticism. We are on our way. Don't touch a thing and tape a big area off."

"I'm sure you do."

"Bye."

DFBI Murdoch asked the question first, "What was that about?"

"The worst imaginable. Here is the condensed version. Two more SCOTUS interns have been killed, run over by a hit-and-run driver. They were with Justice Mary Ruth Nichols; she got a couple of scratches and bruises but seems otherwise to be all right. Cop on the scene doesn't think she was the target."

"Intentional?"

"All the witnesses—and there were apparently a lot of them—agreed that there was no question about it; the three women were the victims of an intentional attack."

"Okay, we'll postpone this to another day. Let's go; forget about traffic laws; I'll make a call to the State Police."

It was lights and sirens all the way across rough dirt and gravel roads, interstates, and city streets, to the crime scene in Colonial Williamsburg in Virginia.

The FBI agents stuck their cred-packs out their car windows and their vehicles were waved through. Everyone ran to the center of the yellow tape and found two bodies lying in black Mopec body bags. Each newcomer to the scene instantly recognized Justice Mary Ruth Nichols sitting huddled on the back of the EMS truck wrapped in a blanket. A woman police officer was just finishing her preliminary interrogation, treading lightly because Judge Nichols look ashen and as if she was about to topple over.

SA O'Leary took over the case and thanked the Williamsburg officer.

"I am sure you were thorough; so, I am not going to do any more than ask a few easy questions. Did she—by any chance—get a license plate number?"

"No, Ma'am, but not for want of trying. She insists that there were no license plates, front or back."

"Doesn't make one immediately conclude that this was just another auto v. pedestrian mishap, now does it?"

"Nope. And the judge would never let you get away with putting such an idea in the report. She is adamant that the driver rounded a corner and aimed right at the three of them. The car had to swerve around several other cars in order to hit them straight on. I believe her."

O'Leary nodded her head and turned away to walk to where the judge was sitting, her head in her hands.

"Headache? Judge?"

"Bad one."

"Are you waiting for an ambulance?"

"Not exactly. I'm sitting on it, and we'll take off as soon as you are done questioning me."

O'Leary skimmed through the report the uniform officer had handed her.

"What kind of car was it, Judge?"

"I don't know much at all about cars, but it was a sedan."

"Make?"

"I don't know one make from another. Sorry."

"Color?"

"Kind of a dirty sickly blue, lots of rust spots."

"Think you could recognize it from a photo array?"

"I probably could."

"How many people in the car?"

"I only saw one. It happened so fast, not more than a few seconds at most."

"Anything stand out about the driver?"

"Not really. He or she was not very big, barely saw the head above the steering wheel. The driver had a slouchy black hat on, like the millennials wear. Long black hair, looked uncombed."

"Race?"

"Not sure. Certainly not dark skinned, not African-American or Indian subcontinent; I am sure of that."

"Asian, Middle Eastern?"

"Possible, but my view was so brief, I could never swear to what the race was. I certainly could never pick the perpetrator out of a line up. If I had to make some kind of judgment, I would go with Asian before Middle Eastern, I think."

O'Leary was getting a bit worried about how the judge was doing; so, she nodded at the EMS driver that it was time to get her to the hospital to be checked out. She dreaded the media firestorm that would break out as soon as she entered the hospital.

"Anything else come to mind, Judge?"

"Only that I have never seen anyone die before. What a terrible thing it was to see the life snuffed out of those two gentle, beautiful, brilliant, girls. They are not statistics, they are women, and very fine ones. Both of them were my interns—Sophie Tuttle, and Claire Jackson. Don't let anyone forget those names and let them just be called 'girls'.

"I am so mad, I could spit. Maybe the scales have dropped off my eyes, but I think I can see the emotions and thinking behind the death penalty. I am a liberal. I remember someone saying that a conservative is a liberal who just got mugged. Maybe there's some truth in that. I wish you success, Special Agent O'Leary."

"And you as well, Judge."

CHAPTER
ELEVEN

With two more "Intern Murders", involvement of a sitting Supreme Court Justice, and a maelstrom of national and international news bombarding the papers, the airways, and the ethernet, and nothing coming from law enforcement or politicians of any benefit, it was time posthumous for the task force exclusive meeting to readjourn in Yellow Breeches Creek.

None of the participants had to be coaxed into coming to the meeting since a sense of desperation, even doom was hanging over them. The killings had to stop; the murderer (s) had to be brought to trial; and SCOTUS had to regain its footing and once again begin to carry on its crucial work for the nation and its people. Several of the justices had hired one or more bodyguards and even demanded their heavily armed presence in the hallowed court room where oral arguments were heard… in what now felt less like recent past and more like the 'good old days'. But not after the spate of Intern Murders began. The murders were affecting the court as did the Covid pandemic in 2020. The building was almost completely shut down.

Sybil said, "Well, my friends, here we are; this is déjà vu all over again."

DFBI Owen Murdoch smiled and said, "and we are not an inch closer than when we started this meeting two days ago. If we are keeping score, it is killers 4 and cops 0, and no promises for improvement on the horizon."

Task Leader SA O'Leary stood up as chairperson and announced, "The meeting is now in session. The agenda has one item, 'How do we find the killer or killers'?"

Clarke Fitzgerald, assistant to the president, was the new man. His appointment to the special section of the task force came at the express behest of the worried president.

Mr. Fitzgerald said, "It is an opportune time to regroup and reassess where we stand. I need to be brought up to date and would greatly appreciate a round of reports about our status. May I suggest that we go about this as debaters in a sense, each speaker touting the evidence for the few scenarios left to us and how they hold up or not."

MacGee spoke up for the first time, "I volunteer to take the thorny political angle as my topic. We all may be seeing it as the 500 pound gorilla in the room that we are afraid to look in the eyes or even mention."

Affirmative nods by everyone else granted MacGee the leeway to continue.

"For most of my life I admit that I have been naive about the Supreme Court. The justices put on the court were given a lifetime tenure because of their incorruptibility, their deep knowledge, love, and honor, for the Constitution and for the law, and they were above the fray—the pettiness of politics. They may have been conservative or liberal before coming to the Court, but after elevation to the great position of justice, they were better than all of that, and the country and the justice system was better for their just presence.

"There is a biblical verse, KJV—Acts 9: 18—'And immediately there fell from his eyes as it had been scales: and he received sight forthwith, and arose, and was baptized'. That applies, I think. I have watched presidents manipulate the court by putting political cronies and persons who will favor their world and governing view. The more I follow the Court, the more the scales fall off.

"So, my first suggestion is that someone or some group wants to send the Court a message. That person or group has suffered damage from a controversial decision."

"How on earth do we locate such people and narrow down the field after that?" Sybil asked.

"Old fashioned cop work but with computers. We round up an army of computer specialists and begin finding likely candidates."

Fitzgerald offered, "I can find dozens of volunteers just by telling them the White House needs their help. They will want to be part of something good going on in Washington."

The DFBI said, "Great. We are too short-handed because of our anti-terrorism mandate to even allow vacations at our place. I like the idea, and we'll help anyway we can."

"MacGee continued, "Sandra Day O'Connor was not only the first woman on the Court, but—over time—she arguably became the most important and influential one because she provided the final 5-4 deciding swing vote on a number of critical and controversial issues even though she was an archconservative. The most contentious were votes that could have led to the Court making abortion illegal. On several such votes, she saved Roe v. Wade, usually on procedural reasons; but she earned real enmity from the right. She is long gone, but we can look at the issues rather than the persons to find people with powerful grudges. She was proof that the number five is the most important number there is for SCOTUS."

"Well, at least that narrows the field of possible suspects somewhat," DFBI Murdoch said. "I'm in favor of anything that makes the practical work a bit less onerous."

"Again SOC was something of a purist about the law itself and used that mindset to make her decisions even if the legal decision or precedent violated her personal moral sense. She was an ardent Roman Catholic and a hidebound Eisenhower Republican right winger when she came to the legal rescue of Roe v. Wade. I'd bet the farm that some Alt Right fanatics wanted her off the court even if they had to assassinate her. We can narrow the field some more to look first at recent cases to find the true believers who believe they have been cheated."

"The Alt-Right began as a newsfeed, *Breitbart*. Proper newsfeeds provide an ideal platform from which to frame people's understanding of themselves and their world, in this case, the white Anglo-Saxon Protestants who have been evolving a victimhood related to losing their former power, position, and income. As part of the normal curatorial function of newsfeeds, judicious editing can easily and imperceptibly morph into deliberate spin, and that is what Breibart and the Alt-Right did."

There was a chorus of head nodding. MacGee was giving much wanted direction to the self-appointed task force within a task force.

"Finally, and then I'll shut up; there is one more area I think bears scrutiny. That is the need to select the hot-button issues of today and find general areas which extremists on either side might find cause to commit murder over. Think of the heat generated by Roe v. Wade, women's rights, inequality for women, or Latinos or Blacks. And don't leave out White Supremacy. Most people see the Alt Right as merely extremist racists.

"But, in the minds of the kluckers, the far-right base, and the left-behind whites in the rust belt and coal country, there is a terrible societal turn against the "white race"; and they are hell-bent on halting that trend. It is reasonable to conclude that—for some—it is worth killing to restore whites to their rightful dominant position in law, society, religion, government and in the workplace. Those areas should keep us all working overtime while law enforcement does what they do best—finding the individual killer or killers. With that, I will yield the podium."

He smiled and the rest of the people sitting around the table in the Yellow Breeches Creek cabin were relieved to have a pragmatic direction to pursue. JPAMJ MacGee's stock went up considerably that afternoon.

CHAPTER
TWELVE

The FBI found a large, well-wired–but little used–basement room for the White House's volunteers to use for their computer blitz to find potential suspects for the Intern Murders. There were private citizens, major company, and government professional hackers—based on the Executive Order of May 21, 2021 "on improving the Nation's Cyber Security" mandating federal agencies to implement multi-factor authentication and encryption for data at rest and in motion. President Duke and US Attorney General Carter Wilson Coppin signed off on the project granting access to privileged information including SCOTUS records.

Specifically, the two primary authorities alerted the White House Industrial Control Systems Cybersecurity, DARPA, CISA [The Cybersecurity and Infrastructure Security Agency], NSA, DHS, DOD, GSA, and seven major private companies with ongoing successful programs. A dozen university professors of computer science volunteered to guide the volunteers and to guarantee the thoroughness and accuracy of the search.

The problem to begin with was not running into difficulty locating potential and believable suspects, but there was a mounting hill of data which was threatening to swamp the computer experts and to render the search too large to manage for the volunteers or for law enforcement agencies.

The members of the task force were deeply concerned that the project was beginning to bog down. City police, FBI, and county sheriffs, were receiving an unprecedented overload of persons of interest to investigate and were all demanding additional money and personnel to handle the load. All this set MacGee to thinking.

MacGee did his best thinking during conversation with his long-time trusted associates, Ivory White and Caitlin O'Brian. He set up a breakfast meeting with them to seek their input and to suggest a rather unusual possible course of action—even for their firm.

Caitlin said, "Hey, Boss, this must be pretty important for you to okay such a great spread."

MacGee said, "It's write-off; and yes, it is 'pretty important'."

Before doing the serious thinking, the three launched a serious attack on the gourmet spread. MacGee had had his FROGS [Front Office Girls] order special favorites for everyone: Eggs Benedict, Bananas Foster, Ricotta pancakes, rum raisin sticky buns, and Belgium waffles with fresh blueberries. He knew where the best coffee was brewed in New York and the finest cheeses which rounded off the great meal.

Ivory patted his stomach and admitted defeat.

"Great breakfast, Boss. Now I'll have to work out double for the next week. What's your newest weird idea that you are worrying about enough to bribe us?"

"Simple. You are aware of the extreme efforts the government and the private sector is going to in order to find a motive, a suspect, and evidence leading to a conviction, in the Intern Murders Case. So far–I am sorry to say–we have not really gotten anywhere. Five people are dead, and I would not be at all surprised to see more. At present, we seem to be powerless to stop the killings. So, I want to propose a somewhat off-the-wall idea to investigate."

"Oh, dear," said Caitlin, "this is probably going to hurt."

MacGee laughed and said, "Could do, could do."

Then he moved right into his plan, one he had been thinking about for days.

Something nagged at the back of Sybil Norcroft's mind, something left undone. The more she thought about it, the more like Russia it all smelled. In the earlier investigation, she had strongly suspected the oligarchs and the criminal syndicate—called Russian organized crime or Russian mafia, otherwise known as Bratva–which is a collective of various organized crime elements originating in the former Soviet Union. The acronym OPG is Organized Criminal Group, used to refer to any of the Russian mafia groups, sometimes modified with a specific name, such as *Orekhovskaya* OPG.

Before, when she deemed the mafia and the oligarchs not to be responsible; Sybil had been particularly careful and thorough. She remained convinced that her first judgment was still correct. After further reflection, she realized that she had committed a very freshman mistake; she had overlooked the nice fellows in the Russian FSB, CVR, and FSO, intelligence services.

In the new investigation she was planning, she would have to very careful not to be discovered. That would result in an international incident and warm the actual perpetrators—if they were Russian—and they would go to ground leaving the US DCIA standing out in the open with egg on her face.

First, she arranged for her old go-to dark-side agents—Mac Young and Lincoln Howard—to meet her in her top-secret area on The Farm—Camp Peary, the CIA training center and home to a special dark prison–where Sybil's favorite serious criminals were held for life.

"Gentlemen, I presume you have had a good rest since our last caper. It's time to get back to work, I think."

Mac Young said, "What more intrigue and mayhem can be left in the spy world, Boss Lady?"

"I have begun to think that the four intern murders are all connected to each other and to an organization which is most likely a state actor. I'd like your opinions about that."

Lincoln spoke first, "I am biased by my career experiences, but I can't see any other answer. I think you and the task force have just about exhausted the other possibilities. But didn't you check out the Russkies and the Chinese yourself, Sybil?"

"I did, but I neglected an obvious—if dangerous even to think about—avenue of approach. Care to guess?"

"State actor?" Lincoln said, "Russia is the first ten choices."

"My opinion exactly," Mac agreed.

"I am going to have to call in some markers, and you guys are going to have to get out your parkas and mukluks; it's cold in Moscow this time of year."

"*Da, da*," the two men chorused and laughed with their director.

CHAPTER
THIRTEEN

The main body of the Intern Murders task force—which had begun to call themselves "The Political Force" as did the two splinter groups—was not convinced by any hypothesis lacking sound evidence. In that majority opinion, the motive had to be political somehow, and all the investigative group needed to do was to look deeper into SCOTUS itself and to evaluate the justices and the enemies they had developed. Chief Justice Daniel George Cabot III was the lead proponent of that hypothesis, and his opinion held a great deal of sway and carried the day when the task force met after the hit-and-run murders of the two liberal interns. His greatest fear was that the monsters who did that would eventually find a way to assassinate a sitting justice, and that gave him serious dyspepsia.

Several members had been influenced by MacGee's salient comments transmitted back from the Yellow Breeches Creek cabin get-together.

The Chief Justice asked for a preliminary report from the unit that was delving into the Supreme Court's records to find potential suspects.

Clarence Danwell–the DARPA wizard with a penchant for wacky ideas—opened the large green covered folder marked "Top-Secret" and began to read sections the unit had highlighted with yellow markers:

"To begin with, you, Sir, as the new Chief Justice, have not been on the Supreme bench long enough to have accumulated serious enemies, in our opinion. We have graded you as having a 1 out of 10 risk of an attack; no one gets a complete bye. So, we will go down the list of justices by order of seniority, longest serving first.

"Senior Associate Justice, Mr. Angus Dagon Zysteric-conservative—although, he is a strong conservative, his few written decisions—either majority or dissident—have been quite tame and rarely written for highly controversial issues. Our risk rating is 2 out of 9.

"The next senior—and the direct opposite of Justice Zysteric is Justice Ruth Nichols, a very outspoken liberal in her opinions on and outside the bench. She has written scores of articles for law school reviews, has spoken out on a variety of favorite topics for liberals and often—if I might say so—in intemperate language.

She has had numerous e-mail threats and threats voiced in right wing rallies, as recently as last week. Strangely enough, there have been more than a few such threats from the progressives' side claiming that she is not liberal enough. We have thus far pegged her as the most likely candidate for a violent attack. 9 out of 10, especially since she has already been involved in a murderous attack, herself.

"Next is Justice Hyrum Parke Hays–a fellow liberal who almost always votes with Justice Nichols–has had his shares of threats, but none nearly as specific as those against Justice Nichols. He has kept his off-the-bench appearances to the minimum. Therefore, we grade him as a 5 out of 9 chance of being a victim.

"Next is Justice Douglass Carlsson a fellow conservative whose main focus is on getting rid of Roe v. Wade, and he makes no bones about that. Women's groups, suburban white males, and African-Americans generally dislike him; and many have openly expressed desires that he would soon die in office. However, there have been no actual threats of harm or murder. We grade him as a 3 out of 9 risk.

"Justice Eric Lund Clifton is a lock step conservative who has a one-hundred percent history of voting for conservative issues and a 100 percent history of voting against liberal ones. His demeanor is placid and agreeable nevertheless; so, he seems not to have engendered many actual enemies. We grade him as another 5 out of 9.

"Justice Karl Damien Rogers, Jr. is a kind of old-fashioned Southern conservative who has always been bombastic and raw in his utterances for the conservative cause. President Duke loves him, but African-Americans hate him. Take your pick of enemies; every organized black group, university professors, and rank and file Duke base Republicans. Ask any one of them his or opinion, and they will tell you that the country would be better off he were to wake up dead one morning or to be involved in a fatal car wreck. However, actual threats have been few and fairly mild. Many of his dissenters consider him to be little more than a harmless old curmudgeon. We grade as having a 3 out of 10 risk.

"Justice Isabela Duncan Parowan is a conservative much like Clifton; she goes along to get along. There have been several times, however, when she has served as the swing vote in the liberal's favor, more like Sandra Day O'Conner in some of her votes. She has always stood in favor of Roe v. Wade; so, the more likely killers from the right are rather confused by her and seldom make threats. We were divided in our opinions of her; so, we ended up with a grade of 3-4 out of 10 without real conviction.

"The lowest in seniority, but nowhere near least in having accumulated enemies is our most recent appointee to the bench other than the Chief himself, and the youngest person on the current roster, our final conservative, Perez Miguel Villarreal, the token Latino, some say; and the man who makes it a seven to two court. There continues to be strong criticism of the president for appointing him with the cloud of "Me-too" complains swirling around his head and for what has been strongly voiced critiques of what is deemed to be anti-woman decisions. Because of the plethora of strongly worded threats from female liberals, and especially progressives, and from central city and suburban white males—possible wannabes—we grade him with a 4 out of 10. That may be too low because of the committee's bias that leans to the concept that women are less violent than men."

Chief Justice Cabot III asked, "So, Doctor Danwell, does your committee have any suggestions for the task force here?"

"Some simple and readily apparent ones. Double the security force night and day in and around the Supreme Court Building until all of this is completely and satisfactorily settled. Put 24/7 security on Justices Nichols and Hays, including their persons, their families, and their residences. And same for you, Chief Justice. It would be too great a coup for someone to strike you for any of us to ignore.

"No one will like this; but, beginning today, place unobtrusive security personnel in the argument hall itself. They should be in mufti and not have a police or military appearance or manner—very similar to the Federal Air Marshal Service. This would be at least until all this is blows over. In my opinion, the role of SCOTUS has elevated to the point that the dangers are equivalent to that facing the president and his Secret Service and should become a permanent fixture."

"Any thoughts on likely perpetrators?"

"Infinity and none, I'm afraid, Chief Justice. It is an unsolved conundrum with too many possibilities and no real probabilities."

"I'm afraid you're right, Doctor.

MacGee paid close attention and had nothing to add to the already vexing Gordion Knot before the law enforcement officers. He was convinced more than ever to go forward with his own plan and to discuss it with the task force only when he became able to add something concrete to the direction for them to head.

CHAPTER
FOURTEEN

T he Supreme Court was very busy as it was always at this point in its session. The early three weeks had concentrated on lesser certiorari and writs of mandamus cases where the interns had written the descriptions and what should be the decision of the Court. It was an exercise for the interns and a chance for them to show what they were made of. The word certiorari comes from Law Latin and means "to be more fully informed." A writ of certiorari—most of which were drawn up by the interns of the justice to whom the case was assigned–ordering a lower court to deliver its record in a case so that the higher court may review it. The US Supreme Court uses certiorari to select most cases it hears. A writ of mandamus is an order from a court to an inferior government official ordering the government official to fulfill their official duties properly or to correct an abuse of discretion. Hence the input of the interns was important and often appeared in the writing of the Court's final decision.

In fact, the Court accepts only about 100-150 of the more than 7,000 cases that it is asked to review each year. Typically, the Court hears cases that have been decided in either an appropriate US Court of Appeals or the highest Court in a given state–if the state court decided a Constitutional issue. The nine justices are cautious and methodical, unlikely to go beyond rulings on narrow facts of a case rather than taking on the whole issue, e.g. Roe v. Wade. One reason for that is writing an opinion is real and time-consuming work: carts and stacks of books and briefs, long hungry, sweaty, hours pouring over manuscripts, open books, and computer screens.

Even that many cases would overwhelm the appointed nine members if it were not for their near slave faithful interns.

The clerks were important players in the judicial schema. They were hired to do research and to help write the justices' judicial opinions. A given justice typically employed four clerks who cull the thousands of petitions for certiorari, and are largely responsible for researching and drafting opinions. The positions are prestigious, sought after by legions of brilliant and experienced applicants; and they pay well. The clerks sign on for a year of working seven days a week often for hours that no union would ever permit, in fact, often until they cannot work anymore for a period.

Chief Justice Cabot III decided during the first weeks of the term that the heavy controversial cases, such as School Prayer, which had raised its shaggy head again because the far right president had pushed it; Roe v. Wade from a disputed Texas federal court ruling; secession of a portion of Northwestern United States and Southwestern Canada—called the Cascadia Secession–with potential boundaries drawn along larger ecological, cultural, political, and economic, boundaries than the original Northern California and Southern Oregon ones; and statehood for Washington DC and Puerto Rico, should be kept back for a time.

All those cases had been simmering along in the federal court system for more than a decade. Cabot III was determined to make his name and to do so promptly; so, he put those thorny items on the docket for December, however brash his colleagues on the Court thought his choices were.

Also–as is usual–there were criticisms in law journals, in law school classes, and on the streets by protestors—the usual crowd. There were critiques and protests for or against every side of every question, which was the general expectation of Court watchers. The difference this year was that there was genuine fault-finding personally for the individual justices and for the Court collectively.

A recurrent complaint was that the justices and the interns from time immemorial had not been chosen from the states and universities west of the Mississippi. The American Conservative Magazine wrote: "Yale, Harvard, Yale, Harvard, Yale, Harvard, Harvard, Harvard, Arizona," a reference to the law school alma maters of the current justices when SOC arrived on the court and had not changed its opinion since. The magazine pointed out that the heartland of the United States never produced a justice or had a justice who had campaigned for or held an elected office, served in a presidential cabinet, or had gone to war. The elitist handle was being placed on the shoulders of the justices and interns by intelligent and educated people of both ideological persuasions.

Another author—who was applauded from both sides—wrote that "Elite schools beget elite judicial clerkships beget elite federal judgeships. Rinse, repeat." The strong perception of elitism resonated in the backrooms of the Republican Base, and the BLM ghetto bodegas.

The Democrats decried the favoritism of the court towards conservatives that would not be able to be changed for many decades owing to the longevity of the justices and their lifetime appointments. Furthermore, it is a given that justices select interns based on how closely the intern matches the justice's legal and social philosophy. Justice Clarence Thomas said: "I won't hire clerks who have profound disagreements with me. It's like trying to train a pig. It wastes your time, and it aggravates the pig."

The Platonic ideal of a disinterested government in truth vanished as soon as an attorney who came to plead his /her client's case, an intern, an associate justice, or the Chief Justice entered the building. The Brethren were not at all immune to political, religious, or ideological, pressure or persuasion, a definite disappointment to true believers who pledged allegiance to the concept of strict constructionist Constitutional law administered by the justices.

But: The Federalist Society—a growing influence—embraces the doctrine of original intent, and textualism insists of literal meaning i.e. as the founding fathers had originally intended their words to mean, not as liberal judges had manipulated it to mean. Originalism—an even stricter concept of how SCOTUS decisions should come from, and one of the tenets of faith of the Alt Right—insisted on the doctrine of original public meaning and purpose of the words of the founding fathers. Breitbart and other Alt Right sources beloved by the Base helped the cause along by supplying "words" of the founding fathers from suspect sources of which the far right was so enamored.

Sybil, herself, decided to go to Russia herself to meet with the small and brilliant group of expert hackers whose extravagant lifestyles had been financed for seven years by her CIA secret funds. They had always produced very useful materials, mostly information which did not add to the ongoing disagreements between the *Rossiyskaya Federatsiya* [Russian Federation] and the eighteen intelligence agencies of the United States. Sybil sincerely hoped that this case would not be an exception, because if the Russian government was directly involved as a state actor in the murder of US federal court personnel, it could hardly be construed as anything but an act of war. Her gut made her highly suspicious of her Russian counterparts and especially of the deeply antagonistic president, Yankil Fedeorevich Naviensky, and his personal coterie of young computer geniuses.

She flew into Moscow Domodedovo Mikhail Lomonosov Airport disguised as a bent over old lady, and she carried the best forged American passport her

CIA experts had ever produced. On a separate flight to a different airport on a different day, Mac Young and Lincoln Howard–her go-to agents when something had to get done–had to be kept an absolute secret, and where daintiness was not an operational requirement, entered the country through St. Petersburg and took the overnight Tolstoy train to Moscow to link up with her.

The two agents had already located the new luxury apartment on 27, building 3, Ostozhenka Street where the hackers had moved in order to enjoy as much decadent capitalistic high life as possible. Sybil and the two large rus (or Visigoth) appearing men were met by a pair of peasants–an elderly man and woman—driving a 1965 olive-drab UAZ Bukhanka off-road van. They clambered into the cargo space quickly, and the Bukhanka with its refurbished engine sped off towards Ostozhenka Street.

Sybil and MacGee had not discussed with each other where they were headed in this late, rather impromptu, point in the investigation of the intern murders. The official task force had reluctantly lapsed into an unwelcome period of thinking for lack of anything obvious that needed doing. McGee, Ivory, and Caitlin, took a trip to Manhattan's Chinatown, next to the lower eastside neighborhood. MacGee knew he was taking a calculated risk, but he did have a marker with one of the American triad leaders, Ding Li Chen, that he intended to call in for collection.

MacGee had been hired by Global International Insurance Consortium to investigate the possibility of fraud by Ding in a series of business transactions between

American and Beijing investors. MacGee obtained information related to grey areas of Ding's family tong that could have obliquely involved Ding himself if revealed. As a matter of friendship, and by letter-of-the-law strict construction of his case, MacGee left that out of his report.

That decision saved Ding Li Chen's clean business life, and the Shanghai Chinese leader ["Dragon's Head] of the transnational crime syndicate—triad or black society—the Long Zi Group who had just wrested control of the Shanghai Triad from its opium kingpin leader Fat "Sleepy" Hung Choi. He owed MacGee, who had refused a monetary payment to avoid any kind of paper trail between MacGee and Associates and the Long Zi Group.

Their tired Uzbekistan cabby made a beeline towards lower Manhattan and Chinatown. He wove expertly through the teeming pedestrian, bicycle, rickshaw, and vehicular traffic, taking the route he knew would take the least time and would attract the least attention. MacGee, Ivory, and Caitlin, took brief notice of the restaurants for dumplings, pork buns, and hand-pulled noodles or the busy sidewalks packed with souvenir stores, bubble tea shops, and markets selling everything from fresh and dried fish, Chinese blue and white pottery, fat Buddha statues, to exotic herbs and spices. Locals were hanging out in leafy Columbus Park for Tai Chi, chess, and mahjong. It was all so peaceful, but MacGee and his associates knew too much about the neighborhood's underbelly to be taken in by the almost scripted tranquility.

The beaten-up faded grey and red gypsy cab pulled into the narrow alley behind the seedy old community center on Division Street in Manhattan and let his fares out. MacGee paid him for the trip and a good tip which was an unspoken way for the man to forget the three of them. The Uzbekistan cabby did not make out an invoice or a receipt.

A 62-year-old Chinese immigrant in a baggy grey sweater and a Mets baseball cap pulled low had been helping elderly–new to America–residents to sign up for free classes where they could socialize, have some gaming fun, and lose their hard-earned and scrupulously saved money to the Long Zi Triad, just as they had done in the old country. The late middle age Han Chinese man spoke no English, although he had carried an American green card for forty-three years. He had never needed to learn the strange sounding American language. He admitted to having one small vice: gambling. His "volunteer" service not only aided the newcomers, but it also helped pare down some of his personal gambling debts owed the paternalistic triad leaders.

The man shuffled over to where the white man and woman and negro man were standing after having alighted from a taxicab.

Held up a sign in English: "MACGEE GROUP"

MacGee replied in Mandarin, but the Chinese man did not make any response; either he was deaf or did not speak the language. MacGee's Cantonese was rough at best; so, he turned to Caitlin.

She gave the man a friendly smile and asked, "*Wǒmen kěyǐ yīqǐ shuō yīngyǔ ma?*" [Can we speak Cantonese together?"]

He gave her a startled look, being unused to hearing any *báirén nǔrén* [white woman] speak his native language, especially with all the correct dialectical nuances.

"I am pleased to do so," he said in a somewhat older style of the language, but still understandable to Caitlin.

Cantonese—or "simplified Chinese"–is a variety of Chinese originating from the city of Guangzhou, Hong Kong, and Southeastern China, with about 68 million native speakers. Unfortunately for MacGee, Cantonese is generally not understood by the dominant Mandarin speakers and vice versa. That notwithstanding, the conversation and Caitlyn's translations facilitated understanding and an efficient brief communication.

"I am asked to bring you to the esteemed and honorable leader of our family organization, Ding Li Chen, who is attending to other guests on the lower floor. Please to following me."

They walked about half a city block to a red door ornamented with gold framing and lettering.

"Please to come this way," the servant said in his quiet servile voice.

He led them to the stairways. They could hear raucous laughter and shouted conversation coming from the smoky second floor. Dominoes, 13-card poker, and mahjong, are the main games. The clacking of mahjong tiles reverberated off the walls of the community association. MacGee and the small party of his friends and their new guide made their careful way into a dimly lit, smoky, dingy, basement-level, parlor from back in the old times of Chinatown.

As they walked and descended the stairs, the guide said he had many friends like him: Chinese immigrants who have limited language skills and aren't interested in fancy cars or expensive dinners. Instead, they sink their winnings into games. They almost always lose, but it is a reassuring reminiscence of the life they had left in China.

He told them a little about the games many played in neighborhood association.

"Many such games," he said, "can run from $1 to tens of thousands of dollars a game, and too many men fail their families by running up debt until they go bankrupt. There are many suicides of bread-winners in our cities. Our good state governor said in a speech that the people of New York should legalize gambling in New York. The government man claimed that it could help generate more than $1 billion in revenue, if you could ever believe what a government official says," the guide said in a voice that had dropped nearly to a whisper.

"It would make life difficult for our Chinese people coming here from Guangzhou who don't know Mandarin and lately from Fujian province who don't speak Cantonese like earlier generations. They have tended to rely on small associations of fellow countrymen from their city for socializing and gambling until they can be part of this large and complicated country.

"No matter what the city or state government says or does, our people will still prefer Chinese games like mahjong and thirteen card poker over roulette, blackjack or those noisy slots."

"Don't you think that would be the end of Chinese gambling here in America, Sir?" Caitlin asked.

"Oh, no, Gentle Lady, Chinese do not much like change. They will find other places just like they do in the PRC. Also–like in the PRC–the triads have people working in the police buildings who have information about crackdowns and will even volunteer people to be arrested…and so this is would only be a repeat of history of a pattern of open and closed eye of tolerance or intolerance of gambling as a vice," he said, "as it has been for thousands of years."

"But, the women are not happy about it. I hear that from women friends in the neighborhood all the time. Their husbands, brothers, uncles, and sons, are gambling and losing their family fortunes," Caitlin said.

"True," the servant said, "In recent days, we have seen for the first time that Chinese women are showing open opposition, raising their voices against gambling as a serious family problem."

Caitlin added, "There are many American families around the country who are having to suffer from gambling addiction destroying their families. It's the same in Chinatown as well, I can see."

The guide led them to the darkest and smokiest corner of the large casino room. There were windows, but they had long since ceased being serviceable for letting in light or for seeing out. The accumulation of greasy smoke, the Chinese habit of coughing up phlegm frequently, and adherent dust and dirt had taken care of that by a past time before any of the present croupiers, floor bosses, drinks ladies, or *dayuloli* ["lit. "chickens", or prostitutes] of the night, were even born.

There, seated at a desk covered with papers, pens, an abacus, and two computers, was a wizened pale man of uncertain age. He had a thin and long face with a wispy mustache and beard that made one think of him as Ho Chi Minh, of Vietnamese revolutionary fame. He wore a dirty grease spotted tee shirt that had dim lettering advertising San Miguel Beer with the words Sham Tseng underneath with a date—1948, barely legible.

Caitlin figured that the shirt had not been washed since that date and probably had been continuously worn during the same period. His linen pants might once have been white, but now they were a mix of grey, brown, khaki, and spots of undetermined origin or time of inclusion. The trousers were tied at the waist with a tightly woven, generally frayed hemp cord.

"*You can't get enough of a good thing,*" she reckoned in the silence of her mind.

"Good evening, my good friend, McGee," he rasped, "what brings you to my humble place of work. Are you and your fine friends out slumming?"

Speaking caused him to accumulate phlegm and a collection of betel nut saliva which required a three-projectile hawking up of brown spit that missed his convenient spittoon every time. It caught Caitlin unaware and caused a wave of nausea to flow over her. She fought the urge to run out and vomit with every fiber of her being.

CHAPTER
FIFTEEN

S ybil, herself, decided to go to Russia herself to meet with the small and brilliant group of expert hackers whose extravagant lifestyles had been financed for seven years by her CIA secret funds. They had always produced very useful materials, mostly information which did not add to the ongoing disagreements between the Rossiyskaya Federatsiya [Russian Federation] and the eighteen intelligence agencies of the United States.

Sybil sincerely hoped that this case would not be an exception, because if the Russian government was directly involved as a state actor in the murder of US federal court personnel, it could hardly be construed as anything but acts of war. Her gut made her highly suspicious of her Russian counterparts and especially of the deeply antagonistic president, Yankil Fedeorevich Naviensky, and his personal coterie of young computer geniuses.

She flew into Moscow Domodedovo Mikhail Lomonosov Airport disguised as a bent over old lady, and she carried the best forged American passport her

CIA experts had ever produced. On a separate flight to a different airport on a different day, Mac Young and Lincoln Howard–her go-to agents when something had to get done–had to be kept an absolute secret, and where daintiness was not an operational requirement, entered the country through St. Petersburg and took the overnight Tolstoy train to Moscow to link up with her.

The two agents had preceded her and had already located the new luxury apartment on 27, building 3, Ostozhenka Street where the hackers had moved in order to enjoy as much decadent capitalistic high life as possible. Sybil and the two large Rus (or Visigoth) appearing men were met by a pair of peasants–an elderly man and woman—driving a 1965 olive-drab UAZ Bukhanka off-road van. They clambered into the cargo space quickly, and the Bukhanka with its refurbished engine sped off towards Ostozhenka Street.

It was the dead of night when the three CIA senior agents reached the posh apartment building on 27, number 3, Ostozhenka Street. They parked the Bukhanka two streets behind and two streets north of Ostozhenka Street. They all checked to be sure that they had not been followed, and the trees and overhanging vines on the street where they parked made the old truck as obscure as it could be. They walked to the apartment building separately and met in the rear among parked cars and trucks, most of them high-end vehicles which would be expected to be owned by senior party bosses, industrial magnates, oligarchs, or smug young Russian hackers, the nouveau riche.

Lincoln fiddled with the rear door lock using his personal favorite H-7LP-7SB [HPC Quick Reset 7-Pin Tubular Lock Pick.]. The lock was a little more stubborn than most of those Lincoln had conquered. It took him three minutes, and then the trio was in the building standing on the high gloss Russian black marble with white veins floor plotting their next move.

"Thirty-second floor," Sybil whispered.

They walked up three floors to the mezzanine to enter the highspeed elevator to avoid the chance encounter with a security guard or some late partying Russian coming back to his or her apartment. They were satisfied that no one saw them. Mac punched number 33 to go past their desired floor; so, they could avoid an unfortunate chance encounter with anyone who might have an involvement with the hackers in apartment 32-1209.

Their luck was holding. They were met with nothing but bright lights and silence. Lincoln checked the door to the stairwell and found it spic-and-span to his liking— very clean, carpeted, and devoid of human beings. He waggled his right forefinger for the other two to follow him, and they slipped into the stairwell and down a floor. Mac was leading at this point and took a quick peek into the hallway. No one. Sybil ran on her rubber-soled shoes to apartment 32. She shook her head in astonishment; the door was ajar, held open by an upturned toe dance slipper.

She hurried back to Mac and Lincoln and whispered, "Door's open. What do you think, is he in there and wants to make a few trips out from time to time, or is he out and is too lazy to lock and unlock? I did not see any sign of security."

"Right now, we're safe," Lincoln said, "who can say about five minutes from now? I vote that we move right in and turn off some lights?"

"Mac?" Sybil queried.

"We have about the same risk whether or not he is in the room at this very moment or out and will return. It seems to that our only problem is noise. I agree with Lincoln, let's go in; but I would strongly suggest that we go in on little cat's feet."

Sybil and Lincoln nodded in agreement.

The door to number 32 was thirty feet away. The three spies ran in their stocking feet carrying their shoes in their left hands.

Mac peaked in. There was no one in the entry room; so, in they went. Sybil looked for any kind of alarm but found nothing. They slipped to the kitchen. No one. Lincoln pushed the door to the first bedroom open and found no one there either. They all stood by the door to the second room and slowly inched the door open halfway. So far, the team had not made a sound, nor had one come from anywhere in the apartment or the building for that matter.

There were two queen size beds in the room, and the floor was littered with empty vodka bottles, strewn clothing, and empty bags of butter and dill crisps, kale chips, empty plastic bottles of cucumber Sprite, Twister Rus Burgers boxes from KFC–with pickled cucumbers–kale chips, stale Plyushka pastry remnants, and for the health conscious, kefir–a mild, slightly alcoholic drinking yogurt.

Each of the two beds held a pair of fully naked boys, limbs akimbo.

"Mac, watch the door for guards or intruders," Sybil ordered. "Lincoln, you take the near bed, and I'll take the far one. Chloroform both of your boys and put plastic cuffs on their wrists and ankles and gag them. I will do the same thing with one of my boys, but the other one is the boy I came to see. He is probably the best hacker in the world, and he works for me. At least, he used to. Quiet now."

Three of the four boys were anesthetized and trussed. Sybil had both agents come to where she was about to wake the fourth boy for a little quiet chat.

Lincoln stood ready to grab the small teenager's wrists and Mac was poised to hold his legs.

Sybil put her right palm over his mouth and whispered, "Dimitri, Dimitri, it's time to wake up."

Whispering was not going to work. Dimitri did not respond, so much as to flick an eyelid.

Sybil knelt beside him and said as loudly as she dared, "*Ochnis', bezdel'nik lenivyy muzhik!*" [Wake up, you lazy no good for nothing peasant!]

Apparently, that sounded like his babushka back in his home village of Okunevo, which the locals believe is the center of the earth. Until the Russian cybertrackers discovered his natural gifts as a hacker, Dimitri Rozitis Radjani, was headed for the firing squad because he was gay.

His eye lids slowly retracted, and he began to register the world around him. It was still cloudy and vague, but the blond woman hovering over him seemed to be someone he knew or remembered or something.

"Wha.., Wha… What's going on? Who're you? Whadda you want? How'd you get into this secure building?"

His speech was gradually becoming clearer, and his thinking more organized. His questions made sense, which was encouraging to Sybil even though she was not very enthusiastic to answer any of them.

She finally answered his questions one at a time and several times each until the conversation began to stick.

"Dimitri, do you want some coffee?"

"Rather have wodka," he slurred back into his Russian accent.

"You have had enough of that rot gut for today. It's time to talk. Here, drink down the whole cup."

It was hot, black, almost as thick as paste, strong as battery acid; and it seemed to be having a positive effect even as he protested its bitter alkaline taste. Perhaps that intentional overwhelming bitterness and nauseating taste was due to Lincoln's efforts to achieve over-extraction, wrong grind size, stale beans, improper brewing, wrong roast, the wrong ratio of water to coffee, dirty equipment, wrong choice of water, and brewing method incompatibility. Otherwise, the agents in the room thought it was perfect.

Sybil knew that Dimitri would not remain lucid for very long when the caustic effects of Lincoln's special brew wore off; so, she pushed him with questions without giving him any rest.

"Who killed the American Supreme Court interns, my friend, Dimitri?"

"Who provided the information the killer needed to find the victims?"

"Was it you?"

"No… then, was it one of the girly boys in the room here tonight?"

"Why does the FSB want to kill our best and brightest young people?"

"Is it some oligarch or general or government stooge you work for?"

"No, you say again and again. How can I believe you? I pay you a great deal of money, and you have ignored me rudely for the past three months. Who is paying you to provide them the necessary information to make the murders possible?"

The battering and brow beating went on for two full and furious hours. His answers were terse and brusque; but they were becoming more cogent as time passed; and his blood alcohol level declined.

Dimitri held up his hand to get his tormentor to stop talking for a moment.

"Listen Snow Queen, we—and by that, I mean the Russians—have had nothing to do with anything happening in your Supreme Court. It is not in our favor to do so at all. Torture me if you want, but I still won't be able to give you any useful information. The Director asked me all your same questions a week ago, and I gave him the same answers. What all of us know is *nichego takogo* [nothing]."

"You know how much I dislike liars, Dimitri…"

"I do, and I have not spoken a single untruth. I swear it on my beloved grandmother's life. Do you realize how late it is? It is nearly three o' clock in the morning. If the FSB catches you here, they'll torture you for the fun of it, and they'll put a ring in your nose and lead you like a dumb ox all around the world to show how foolish the American CIA is. Get out… Now!"

The CIA agents knew they were not going to get anything more useful out of Dimitri, most likely because he really did not know anything.

Mac and Lincoln looked Sybil in the eyes.

"Okay, we're out of here. Dimitri, you know how painful the Snow Queen can be when she's been double-crossed. If your memory improves, do give me a message—same phone number.

The Americans left the way they came in having likely learned something out of the fiasco: the Russians probably did not have any involvement in the intern murders.

CHAPTER
SIXTEEN

S ybil Norcroft was thoroughly displeased that the effort to find the SCOTUS intern killers—the so-called "Intern Murderers"—had so completely bogged down. She blamed herself as much she did anyone else. She began to doubt that the army of US law enforcement officers had left any hate group out of their search, or that any clandestine search of the Eurasian continent would produce results either. She had narrowed her choices—by wont of getting any workable clues from looking at known criminals or other usual suspects, at crime syndicates, or known individual loony-tunes or on-line haters, was going to pan out.

After her deep search in the usual world-wide haunts of America haters and religion-based terrorists and their sheltering countries and organizations, she found herself gradually coming to the conclusion that the source of the murders was not likely to be state-sponsored per se.

She scratched her head for an answer and; by serendipity, she decided that maybe the answer might lie among some of the behind-the-scenes actors who had long harbored antipathy against the United States and also against their countries' leadership. Or—maybe it was simpler than that—if all else fails, follow the money.

She arranged a conference call with Mac Young and Lincoln Howard.

"Hi, guys, I have been brain-storming about this Intern Murders thing; and I have come up with some more ideas for us to pursue."

"The 'us' to whom you refer would not be named Mac and Lincoln, would it, Boss Lady?"

"It crossed my mind, I have to admit, Lincoln."

"How far did it get?" Lincoln responded facetiously.

"To the finish line. Glad you asked. I have a list of men for you to meet and to question. Pull out all stops, because I want answers. This mission is becoming too much like the hunt for Beelzebub, but the nice vice-president is still in prison; I checked yesterday morning."

"We're paying attention, Boss. What specifically do you want us to do?

"Come to my office on the ninth floor this afternoon about five, okay? Come through the back door. It's that kind of op, I'm afraid."

The face-to-face meeting was business and brief, nearly to the point of being brusque and harsh.

"So, to conclude our pleasant get-together, my friends, the Russians would seem to be out of the running. I want you to be vigorous with the financial genius of the Society of the Muslim Brothers aka The Muslim Brotherhood, namely one Adem Özdemir, who resides right now in a part of Turkey not so well known to the two of you. The Turkish AKP aka AK Parti [*Adalet ve Kalkınma Partisi* or Justice and Development Party] is the ruling party of Turkey which very publicly supported the Muslim Brotherhood after the overthrow of the Muslim Brotherhood-affiliated Egyptian president Mohamed Morsi in July, 2013. There have been some ups and downs, but the AKP is still very much in favor."

"Does your computer full of names and addresses happen to have this Özdemir's particulars? I have always been curious about how that funny looking 'Ö' was pronounced. I think you did right well on that."

Sybil gave a small, theatrical curtsy, to the amusement of her ever-faithful pair of agents—and friends.

"Here is his address in Cappadocia, far eastern central Anatolia, Turkey. The village of Yassıhöyük is a few kilometers outside Gordion, the one where Alexander the Great cut the knot with his sword and where good King Midas ruled. In that busy little village, hiding on Sakariya River Road, number 342 near the cutoff to Yassıhöyük, is the modest home of the vastly important Muslim Brotherhood financial minister Adem Özdemir. Do not announce yourselves. He is known to be both violent and skittish; after all, he is a true believer.

"Your next visit will be to Al Khums, Libya to have a sit-down with our old friend from the war, Haqq Amer Sherif; 26 Qabīlat al Qanawāt; more about that later. Ring me when you have squeezed the necessary juice out of Adem. Please."

Ding Li Chen, in DC Chinatown spoke softly, looking every bit the hide-bound Confucian that he was, "Is this the time of asking for a favor, one to equal the unfortunate experience with the Global International Insurance Company, my dear friend?"

"I deem it to be so; but, it will remain to be seen according to the effort that you and the family tong put out?" McGee said.

"Tell me, my son, what so troubling to you, and how I can be of assistance?"

"My problem is this my erudite mentor, there have been four heinous murders of fine young people, the best our country can produce. They all worked as what we call interns at the Supreme Court, and the important mandarins of the country are angry. They are looking for heads to chop off."

"How would I know of such unpleasant things McGee? Surely…"

"Of course, no one with any sense suggests that you or the members of the family tong share any guilt with the perpetrator or perpetrators. What we ask, and in with full sincerity and seriousness—is that you use the global reach of your business contacts to seek out persons with possible knowledge of the crimes I have described. Perhaps someone has seen someone or something or heard a bit of related gossip. You know how people do talk in the cafes, the Tai Chi exercises, or at the casino tables. We would hope that you could pass such things along to us."

"Hmmh, I see. I will do what I can as a favor to you. I do recall that I, too, once came to you asking a favor;

and you were most gracious. It is what friends do. You can expect a telephone call or to receive one of my messengers with news in the not far distant future. I hope that will be of help."

McGee sipped a little of his fragrant Guangzhou Monkey-Picked Oolong Chai and had to agree with the waiter that the legendary tea was a classic and unforgettable experience, then said, "Dear Old Friend, please never think that I come seeking a quid pro quo. I am your humble friend, and I seek a righteous favor, the accomplishment of which will bring much favor upon you, upon your good family, and your beloved ancestors."

In less than a week, McGee and associates had a name, address, and some particulars that were promising. Immediately upon receiving Ding Li Chen's courier, the three senior associates of the private investigation firm made flight plans to travel overnight First Class on Air China to PEK [Beijing Capital International Airport].

The meeting with Wei Liú Huáng was three city blocks from the Ministry of State Security in the northwest of Beijing in the Xiyuan area [lit. Western Park] next to the Summer Palace in Haidian District. It had taken some name dropping, such as Sybil Norcroft and Ding Li Chen, to grease the skids; but overall, preparations went quite smoothly. It was a bright sunny day, and the tourists were out in droves for their first and only opportunity to see the great treasures of the Peoples Republic of China. That created a chance to hide easily in plain sight, since the American spies blended in with the excited families from all over the world who paid them no attention. Even the MSS agents prowling the squares and streets ignored them.

Wei Liú Huáng [his real name] was the deputy director of Bureau Number 8, Counterintelligence, responsible for monitoring, investigating, and potentially detaining, foreigners suspected of counterintelligence activities. The Bureau primarily covers and investigates diplomats, businessmen, and reporters—foreign and domestic. The bureau's reputation is that it knows everyone and everything, and no one knows a thing about it. DCIA Sybil Norcroft was a decided exception to the latter part of that reputation and arranged the meeting for McGee and associates and for them to receive any and all intel turned up in Wei's endeavors.

Mr. Wei—as he insisted on being called—had been recruited by Sybil herself and had not been particularly difficult to persuade. He was the best and most reliable kind of turncoat agent because his soft point was money. He did it to keep himself and his family living on the scale of the upper middle class of China, even though his career prospects were limited by his lack of direct social contacts with the upper crust of MSS society. His information had always been top drawer; and for that, Sybil trusted the information he gave, if not the man himself.

The meetings of CIA agents and Mr. Wei were usually arranged so that they took place in a different location once a month, each time in a different location and never on the same day of the week or date of the month. This meeting was an exception and described as "urgent" to Mr. Wei who learned that three different Americans whom she trusted would take her place and that of Mac Young and Lincoln Howard. It was in the back room of an attractive side street dim sum place four blocks from the Summer Palace in Haidian District and three blocks from the MSS headquarters called *Bei JingDaXue* [Bo Xing Di Café].

Caitlin entered first, followed ten minutes later by Ivory, and three minutes after that, by the dapper English businessman, McGee. None of them greeted each other or acknowledged Mr. Wei when he arrived. They ordered an assortment of dim sum dishes from passing waitresses including *Bei JingDaXue* house wantons, Chaozhou fenguo dumplings, curry sesame balls, roasted pork rice rolls, cabbage-wrapped shrimp shumai, Chinese pearl meatballs, beef cake, and egg rice, and for dessert, lychee black tea ice-cream. At separate points during the leisurely meal, the four all casually ended up at one table, Mr. Wei's.

"Greetings Mr. Wei," said McGee, we have not met; but we have a close friend–the attractive blond woman– which is why we presumed upon your good nature to meet and dine with you this afternoon. It is a splendid day in Shanghai for a meeting."

The mistake of saying "Shanghai" instead of "Beijing" was the agreed upon password, and the correct response was, "Oh, Sir, you must be tired. If this is Tuesday, we must be in Beijing."

It was actually Monday, which led to a hearty laugh.

Pallid chit-chat was all that took place as long as they were eating, and the waitresses busied about in the room seeing to it that the patrons were well-fed, comfortable, the table cleared, and the bill was paid. Then–per the well reimbursed manager's instructions–they stayed strictly away from the closed-off room.

"We need your resources, Mr. Wei. You—no doubt—have heard of the killings of our young people who serve as interns in our Supreme Court. We have been as thorough as we possibly can to find a motive and to identify suspects. We have a very great many persons of interest; but, legally speaking, no individuals or groups who rise to the level of outright suspects.

"We ask your assistance to find anyone from anywhere with possible motive or opportunity, or means, to carry out such blatant and risky missions. Our leader wishes to divorce herself from the day-to-day activities of my association and any others outside the United States. We cannot be seen to be 'colluding' with Chinese, Russians, Arabs, or radicals of any kind. I am sure you understand."

"Unless there are Chinese nationals—and I strongly doubt it—the search will be lengthy, and I will have to create a plausible legend. If it involves persons outside our purview, the time and costs will increase greatly. I am happy to help, but I must be extremely careful. The consequences for failure on my part are much more than they are on your part."

"Good, and thank you, Mr. Wei. I travel to Asian countries, including the PRC, on a fairly frequent basis; so, you can let my office know that the CEO of "Guanzhou-Zhongsan Urban Construction Company, Ltd" asks for a representative to meet him in the Hong Kong office."

"Is that a genuine company, Mr. McGee."

"It is. And it has never had a bit of trouble with the CCP [Communist Party of China]."

"That is even better. I have had good tidings from an old friend from the revolution days, Ding Li Chen, which has inspired trust in you and in your mission. You may expect a call in a week to ten days. Good day."

CHAPTER
SEVENTEEN

Mac Young and Lincoln Howard landed in Ankara's LTAC [Ankara Esenboğa Airport] just as the sun began to rise in the west—at least that is what it seemed to the two travel befuddled spies as they fought with their own minds to deal with the jet lag, time change—six hours forward–the culture and language shock, even the writing on signs was indecipherable, and the barren terrain devoid of helpful landmarks.

The next task for them was to rent a car. That was easy, since Ankara is as modern as any US city. Uncertain of what their travel was going to entail, they selected a comfortable and powerful Mercedes G 550 SUV with a 4.0L V8 biturbo engine and tires suited for sand and mud.

"Yes, it's expensive, and beautiful, and classy; but we need this work vehicle for three reasons," Mac told Lincoln. "First, it is rugged and can handle any terrain; second, take note that all of the taxicabs are Mercedes—that should tell you something, the way they beat up their cars; and third, Uncle Sugar is paying for the ride with this nice black credit card; and he does not care about the cost, just our safety and comfort."

Lincoln laughed and said, "You are full of it, Mac. But I can't dispute your logic."

The fifty-nine mile drive to the Gordion archeological site by curving–and several times reduced to sand–roads took three hours including a stop for gas, one for map reading, and one for a rest stop, even though they could not locate a rest room. It took little extra time; they were men, after all.

The terrain was an incredible and monotonous volcanic moonscape interrupted with lavishly decorated cave churches, homes, workshops, carved out towering rock formations such as fairy chimneys, and cave hotels, created by men long ago out of the rock formations that emerged due to a geological process that began millions of years ago. Ancient volcanic eruptions blanketed the region in thick ash, which later solidified into a soft lithified volcanic tuff and ignimbrite rock [Ignimbrites are made of crystal and rock fragments in a glass-shard groundmass]. The natural forces of wind and water erosion affected the deposited ash so that only the harder elements were left behind to form the 'fairy chimneys' stretching up to 130 feet into the sky.

It was a good time to come: a sunny but not overly hot day; the crowds of tourists had already gone before them to the archeological site in Yassıhöyük village which held down the dust from tourist busses on the last leg of the trip and provided needed obscurity for the two spies. The last outpost of population of any size was the town of

Gordion—where Alexander the Great hacked through the Gordion Knot with his sword to make himself the King of all Asia Minor. Gordion was rather easily accessible via road or rail to small Polatlı–just over an hour's bus ride from Ankara. No one paid the slightest attention to the two men. The last 18 km to their destination was via a rutted dirt and gravel country road to Yassıhöyük village where it was said that the residence of the vastly important Muslim Brotherhood financial minister Adem Özdemir sat on the eastern bank of the Sakariya River.

The village of Yassıhöyük was a busy little place owing to the large University of Pennsylvania archeological project with all its scientists and support staff, and the daily hordes of tourists from all over the world who came to see the famous archeological works and to wait for near dusk to see the surreal landscape of carved-out towering rock formations which change color with every sunset.

Mac and Lincoln had several hours to kill; so, they joined the tourists for both archeological tours. The first was through the fine little museum built and supplied with artifacts by the visiting archeologists and the townspeople who worked on the digs and took pride in their work. The second tour was to the Citadel, the mound where a king was interred, judging by the votive articles discovered in the man-made hill. It was widely believed–including by the archeologists– that the occupant was the iconic King Midas who ruled Phrygia in the late 8th century BCE. It was a nonstressful and even educational way to spend the eight hours Mac and Lincoln had to pass before starting their work after dark.

The sunset was all it was cracked up to be; as the sun slowly dropped below the horizon, the hoo-doos and other formations went through a series of colorful changes, ranging from yellow to yellow-orange, to deep orange, to orange red, and finally the sun dipping over the edge of the horizon as a red ball. The enthralled tourists all clapped in their own languages, and Mac and Lincoln joined them.

Yassıhöyük village was not a place with streetlights to alleviate the coming darkness, nor was it a locale where there was a long twilight. The two men ate a light supper consisting of local fare: *yaprak/sarma* [vine leaf rolls with filling], *börek* [baked or fried pastry with filling], *Gözleme* [pancakes with greens], *tahini* [sesame paste], traditional cheese, soups with vegetables and legumes, *Manti* [Turkish Ravioli], and meatballs with sauce cooked in clay pot. The fare was good, filling and needed, at the closing of a long day without food.

They started their work when the region was cloaked in full darkness. The two spies had found Özdemir's house during the daylight hours and returned by car, driving without the Mercedes's headlights. They parked a mile from the house in a narrow turnout on the river road where the sides of the road were overgrown with scrub brush. They loaded up their weapons and walked in the deep shadows to number 347. The home was not difficult to distinguish from others around it because people were milling about in the well-landscaped front yard exhibiting no fear or attention to security during what appeared to be a family event.

Unlike any of the neighbors, about a dozen women were working to cook and serve the children and males at the Özdemir house. All the women were cloaked in heavy black burkhas with only eye slits to indicate that there were human beings inside. It was like looking at a spooky horror movie with walking dead or evil spirits moving about without touching the ground. Several dozen children were playing in a manner comparable to pantomime because they were silent, even as they ran about. It was a surreal and unpleasant scene for the nonMuslim spies lurking in the dark and gave ample evidence that this was the dwelling of a hardcore Muslim Brotherhood senior officer.

Özdemir made things a little easier for the two CIA spooks. He framed himself in the light of the large house and appeared to be talking to a pair of younger underlings that neither Mac or Lincoln recognized from the dossier of photos they had studied in preparation for the mission. Özdemir himself was easily recognized by his portly girth and for the fact that he was head and shoulders taller than his companions. It was known that he stood 6'5" tall and weighed nearly 300 pounds—a fact that he used to bully his wife, children, underlings in the brotherhood, and politicians, he encountered. He had been instrumental in bringing down former Egyptian president Mohamed Morsi.

Their first reconnaissance of the house and its grounds revealed a surprisingly small number of security guards, all of whom were seen to be committing the two cardinal sins of security guarding: everyone of them was smoking; and none of them was paying attention. Their concentration was on flirting with the black spook girls, sampling the splendid buffet fare, or napping in the lawn chairs.

Mac and Lincoln waited until a guard left the house and announced in Turkish that the party was over, and everyone should return home "as proper Muslims should do."

While attention was centered on the grounds as the guests departed, the two CIA special agents slipped through the unlocked rear door and hurried up the spiral staircase and found the bedroom obviously belonging to the Lord and Master. They darkened the room and waited.

Özdemir obeyed his own curfew. It was crucial to the cause that he—as one of the foremost leaders—should obey the Islamic orders in every jot and tittle. He opened the door to his bedroom and bade his guards a good night with a final order to them to *Kur'an'a uyun, şedada okuyun ve yatsı okuyun.* [Obey the *Qur'an*, recite the shadada, and give the *isha*—the last prayer of the night.]

He stepped into the room and murmered the shadada in a soft voice as he had done hundreds of thousands of times during his seventy-two years on earth, "*La ilaha illa Allah wa-Muhammad rasul Allah.*"

Lincoln's large and powerful hand cupped over the big Turkish man's mouth, and Mac kicked his legs out from under him.

To prevent him from being able to guess the origin of his assailants, Mac spoke to Özdemir in the Afghan accented Arabic he had used when serving in that poor benighted country.

"Do not make sounds. Do not struggle. If you are quiet and answer our questions truthfully and quickly, you will be able to say the isha and go to bed unharmed. If you do not…"

CHAPTER

EIGHTEEN

McGee, Caitlin, and Ivory–using false passports supplied by the US Department of State's Bureau of Intelligence and Research [INR] and cleared by D, PM, and S/ES-O MilAd–traveled from New York City to Toronto to Reykjavik. From there, the three supposed exchange professors, under the aegis of AO [The Office of Analytic Outreach]–took a secret State Department Boeing 747 flight specially arranged for the three of them to Tangshan Sannvhe Airport, Tangshan, Fergrun District, Hebei, 86 miles from Tiananmen Square.

The Office of Analytic Outreach tailors analytic exchanges to align with and contribute to Department of State and Intelligence Community (IC) analytic and policy priorities. AO analytic exchanges offer new perspectives and analytical insights to thousands of IC analysts and U.S. Executive Branch policy makers. In performance of its regular duties, analytic exchanges prepare State Department officials at all levels, to formulate and advance U.S. foreign policy. All valid AO analytic exchanges are for USG Executive Branch officials. Nevertheless, they are off-the-record and not for attribution to ensure an environment conducive to candid discussion. Or, in this case, to keep the Department of State's clandestine purposes under wraps and to avoid any potential implication of the major independent agencies, the ODNI and the CIA.

The purpose of the intense secrecy for the mission and its civilian contractors was to avoid any prior notice to Beijing's governmental officers or its lower stratum of intelligence officers. In point of fact, the upper echelon officers of the PRC, the CCC, and the MSS, were fully informed and expecting the three Americans. A small–but superbly trained and fully informed unit of the MSS–Beijing Military Region, "Oriental Sword"–is a PLA Ground Force SOF [Special Operations Force] unit. All 3,000 soldiers in this unit can complete all types of operations and are regarded as the elite arm of the country.

Li Zuocheng–General of the People's Liberation Army (PLA) of China, and the chief of the Joint Staff Department of the Central Military Commission–accepted the request by Admiral Jonas Stark Monroe, the Chairman of the JCS of the US. The president of the United States and the Core Leader of the PRC and the CCC had both agreed to the joint venture as being mutually beneficial.

The mission was to investigate the possible perpetrators of the Intern Murders identified by Ding Li Chen, the Dragons Head of the Long Zi Group of the Shanghai Triad, and to bring them to an established interrogation center in Tanghai Town Hebei province—known to a very few people in the world as a CIA Black Site–for McGee and Associates to extract the information that would bring the entire criminal conspiracy to heel. It was of no great import which country or agency took final possession of the criminals. For his part, McGee rather hoped that the PRC would get them. Apparently, their judicial system and prisons were less desirable for the criminals than the American system.

MacGee, Ivory, Caitlin, General Li, and Colonel Ching of the Oriental Sword unit, sat down to munch on items from a generous platter of healthy light Hebei cuisine—choices of steamed dumplings, Moo goo gai pan, baked salmon, and Happy Family–a dish that combined baked chicken, beef roast, and steamed shrimp with fresh vegetables in a light brown Chinese sauce. The food was quaffed down with generous quantities of Snow Beer, Brave the World Series, Shenyang Province's favorite. The brew is so named because of its rich and white snowy foam and flower-like aroma. It has been the best-selling Chinese beer brand for years because of its fresh and refreshing taste.

"That is very good stuff," Ivory said, and looked with yearning at the full pitcher still beckoning to him from the tabletop.

"Enough of pleasure," announced the general. "Time to become serious. Col. Ching, please outline your plan of action."

Col. Ching and the first class master sergeant of the command put up an action map with the mansion compound of the "Big Crocs" as Core Leader dubbed them and why he had declared open season on the billionaires whom he considered to be the equivalents of Russia's oligarchs. The origin of the slur was apt: the Chinese oligarchs live extremely well enjoying lurking in shadows and pulling strings below the surface. The big crocs arose during the booming and corruption-ridden 1990s and 2010s. They deliberately kept their business background vague and business empires remarkably opaque. For the common folk in China, they have a dash of mystery to their legendary standings in China's private sector.

Dragon's Head Ding's dossier and that of Wei Liú Huáng, were more than adequate to condemn the big crocs for a laundry list of major crimes, and they were no cronies of Xi, as the oligarchs are to the president of Russia. The Hong Kong and Shanghai triad chiefs to whom Ding had appealed for information saw the crocs as privileged competitors and opponents and were only too willing to bring them to heel. The triad spies had discovered the Hubei compound and provided photographic and private social media evidence of the chief conspirator being the richest man in all of China, Xiao Jianfeng.

MSS had delved into the recent activities of the big crocs and found very interesting parallels: all of them had met in Singapore a year ago, and again just before the first intern murder; several of them had used the dark net to find reliable and expendable hit men and women; and most damning was that they all attended a very secret, very secure, meeting in the Banyan Tree Macau Hotel the night before the murder of the American jurist, Senior Associate Justice Angus Dagon Zysteric. The most important piece of information the Long Zi Group triad shared with the MSS (for a consideration) was that for the next three days, the big crocs involved in the killings in America were to meet in Xiao's compound, ostensibly to plan the next and most terrible attack—which had the potential to plunge the world into something close to World War Three.

Col. Ching spent a little over an hour laying out the plan of attack on the compound. As he was doing so, auxiliary units filtered into the room—medical team, fire control unit, media unit, and MSS officials ready to send live reports back to the Politburo Standing Committee and to the Office of the Core Leader. When Col. Ching finished his didactic presentation, the action units drilled for two more hours to be certain that everyone was sure of his or her separate role and the collective coordinated action plan.

CHAPTER

NINETEEN

Zhang Wenzhong's compound: The attack commenced at 0500 while the world was still dark, the main force in the compound was still asleep, and presumably, most of them were heavily hungover. The Oriental Sword commandos accompanied by McGee and Associates bringing up the rear to defend US and Sybil Norcroft's interests moving in close on the heels of the commando force. They were spurred on by the knowledge that they were going to be handsomely paid–McGee had to admit to himself–for all the "God and Country" bravado that had preceded the actual mission of the day.

The eight compound sentries were easily taken out by the commando spearhead unit, followed by a unit of six men who threw grappling hooks over the top of the walls and scaled the barriers with practiced ease. They neutralized the electric current coursing through the razor wires and cut through them with Greenlee High Security Metal Truck Seal & Bolt Cutter kits. They dropped into the compound leaving behind sturdy nylon rope ladders on both sides of the wall. Three units of spearhead units cut a total of six entry points before the unit leader tapped his signal mike to inform Col. Ching that entry was now secured, compliments of him and his unit members, a small joke between the two officers.

The rest of the commandos streamed efficiently into the compound and laid out on the ground to make themselves as oblivious to any onlookers as possible. Col. Ching sent two of his men to reconnoiter the perimeters of the compounds buildings before committing his force to full action. McGee, Caitlin, and Ivory, quietly applauded the military precision and performance of the Chinese units as the action began to commence.

Col. Ching gave one last look of his own, then tapped his shoulder mike three times to signal the beginning of the attack proper. There was a short lag time to give the arrest and extraction unit time to assemble by the sleeping quarters of the most important "big crocs." It was imperative that those bigger-than-life criminals all be taken alive if at all possible. Their shame and loss of face was crucial to the PRC's need to show that it had acted very responsibly to rid the world of an imminent threat rather than being a state sponsor of terrorism against the US. Core Leader Xi had an elaborate show trial for the Chinese people and the world audience already.

The interior guards for the big crocs were alert and doing their jobs, but the Oriental Sword troops were better at doing theirs. No sound–so much as even an errant cough or the snapping of a twig–produced the warning the guards would have needed to know that they were under attack. McGee and Associates were impressed by the finesse being demonstrated by the extremely fit and well-trained Chinese commandos, and they were determined that the firm would not prove to be the weak link in the attack team in even the most minimal way.

The sleeping quarter commando unit signaled that they were inside the sleepers' rooms and prepared to execute their orders: take full control of the guards and the big crocs without making noise, or alerting the rest of the compound of lesser importance criminals.

Col. Ching signaled with two rapid succession clicks, and the men in the sleeping rooms flew into action. Every sleeper was chloroformed, and every guard was subdued in silence with six unfortunate resulting deaths that could not be avoided. The sleeping big crocs were trussed and gagged, then the unit leader signaled back to Col. Ching that their part of the operation had been successfully completed.

There remained the ex-fil of the perpetrators and the maintenance of safety and security of the Oriental Sword troops, all in an atmosphere of utmost secrecy. Extraction of the newly acquired big croc prisoners was then only a matter of logistics made a little more difficult by the darkness of the starless, moonless, light in the cloudy night.

Col. Ching pondered and discussed the minor issue of transporting all the security personnel arrested in the sting operation. There were not enough vehicles, drivers, or guards, among the MSS and Oriental Sword troops. Caitlin—with her down-to-earth logic—pointed out the simple solution.

"You have to get the contraband back to Beijing along with the criminals and their criminal security team members. You are now the proud owner of a fleet of new ultra-large, currently empty, made-in-China, Hi-Ace vans."

"Sounds Japanese," replied Col. Ching, just to be picky.

"It does," said Caitlin, "but they are made in China by Jinbei Motors as the Jinbei Haise, King Long Motors, and the Foton Motor Company—all the same Chinese company. Also, note the perfect camouflage: red background, company logo with qing [nature's color—green or blue, greenish black] background and black lettering with a small, but vivid, Chinese Five-starred Red Flag [A large golden star within an arc of four smaller golden stars, in the canton, on a field of Chinese red] symbol on top. And you know that red is one of the lucky colors. And… the company name-JIANFENG-emblazoned along both sides. Perfect!"

"You know how hard it is for a Chinese man to admit that a mere woman is right, Ms O'Brian?"

"Oh, kind colonel, I had never heard such a thing."

They both had a good laugh, as they transmitted the orders to the military and MSS crews. The McGee and Associates contingent begged off from anything that indicated their very-American involvement and left Beijing via the State Department 737 while the Chinese, including Core Leader Xi, posed in front of the cameras of the world lauding their complete and solo success in discovering, arresting, and planning, a mass trial of the "big crocs" the following month.

Everyone was happy from all the countries involved—with the notable exception of the "Big Croc" billionaires and their families. Anonymity served the purposes of most of the entities involved; so, they were happy that Leader Xi could have his day of glory. The Americans were overjoyed that the national nightmare was over; it was enough for them. The three McGee associates were awarded the Presidential Medal of Honor for their role—unspecified—in the Intern Murders solution.

MacGee was asked to present an in-depth explanation of what had brought this all about, and to give his opinion to the United States government and the general public—with appropriate redaction of the sensitive material. It was a great day for the McGee firm.

CHAPTER
TWENTY

The president, CIA, FBI, State Department, US Military, and all Chinese participants in the Intern Murders closure, were understandably reticent to speak out publicly. So, they were happy to have that public duty fall to a nongovernment, nonmilitary, nonintelligence agency, person, and one who commanded national and even international respect. JPAMJ McGee stood before the House of Representatives podium to address a joint assembly of both chambers, the Supreme Court, and the Joint Chiefs of Staff, to deliver an Agatha Christie type denouement of the whole affair. It was expected to be satisfying, thorough, and detailed, and to omit the role of the major players involved in the finale. He humbly wondered if he was up to it all, but the Speaker was now introducing him to the world.

"… Joseph Patrick Aloysius Michael John McGee, to give us all a clear understanding of the whole sorry affair."

His trembling and self-doubts evaporated as soon as MacGee began to speak.

"Madam Speaker, Mr. President, Mr. Majority Leader, Chief Justice Cabot III, members of the Congress and the Senate, foreign dignitaries, fellow Americans, and friends and neighbors… this is a singular honor to address this historical and august body and the people of United States of America and all the good people of the world. This is especially directed to those around the world who were crucial to the solution of this calamity which befell us all. I give my condolences, and I have the temerity to speak for all the world to do that to the families left behind after these heinous crimes.

"To be as clear as possible within the constraints imposed by national and international security requirements, I shall start from the beginning. Someone told me that I was going to play the role of the world's Agatha Christie to unravel the Gordion Knot these crimes constituted. I'll do my best," he said with a self-deprecating smile.

"Up until the first Monday in October this year, the Supreme Court of the United States, opened its doors to usher in a new year's session of dealing with the nation's most vexing legal issues. That evening, a gala celebration was held at the Metropolitan Club in Washington DC. That evening and for many weeks thereafter, the celebratory mood was ruined and put aside. Two very special young men–Court interns, Glen Lincoln Dastrup and Neal Crenshaw Gabler–were brutally and senselessly murdered. A national and international investigative blitz was declared, and every resource of the country and our friends around the world was brought to the task. In brief, that led nowhere.

"We paid particular attention to the possibility that the Court or individual justices had enraged some unstable person or over-heated partisan group. We combed through the archives of debates and decisions, including documents penned by interns. We separated conservative from liberal or progressive opinions held by the victims. We went beyond the Court itself and into social, religious, and political life, and speeches given outside the Court proper. We looked at the transcripts and videos of the Senatorial committee meetings during the advice and consent. We investigated–as much as possible–any credible serious differences of opinion or personal animus between sitting members and did so for the period of the past twenty years. We turned over every stone and looked into every secret we could identify to determine if there was a potential motive for murder, even if it was a crazy one. We talked to members of all races, creeds, and ethnic backgrounds, and especially to their organizations and PACs.

"At the risk of giving offense to anyone on the Court at present or in the past, let me tell you that we spared no one, nor did we favor anyone; we simply sought the truth. We discovered a number of things about the court: it consists of members who are at their core, still people; and they do not always operate on a higher plain. Politics does affect decisions. Tempers do flair. The justices have been known to be petty, profane, even ignoble, at times. Take just the example of slavery. The Court has failed to solve several issues vexing We the People over the past thirty years by their 'start low and go slow' modus operandi and their intentional practice of avoiding firm decisions in very controversial cases. Take Roe v. Wade—The Court's irresolution over Roe v. Wade bred the field for still more cases to be looked at strictly to find narrow fine points to decide upon rather than to decide the issue once and for all and to face up to the firestorm of criticism. Issues as diverse as sex, religion, and the power of the federal government, are other prime examples. The court's opinion bows deeply to conformity.

"Let us all understand that the Court is not a democratic institution; no justice has ever been elected by the vote of the people. As a result, they are not accountable to the people or even to the president who nominated them or the party in power that confirmed the appointment. It has been abundantly clear that the court sometimes caters to the will of the people and sometimes not. That creates a paradox and a conundrum. It also inflames tempers. It fosters grass roots political rebellions. Note the evolution of the court from a leftist leaning institution thirty years ago to an arch-conservative one of today. What do we, the investigators, conclude about that?

"The Court operates largely in secret, and our nation has suffered mightily over the course of its existence from the secrets of a privileged few. When the United States Supreme Court decides a case, nearly all the decision-making process takes place in secret. Their demeanors and personalities are different, and each of them has offended someone who disagreed with them at one point or another. Someone wise to the inner workings of the secretive Court, characterized them as 'Nine Scorpions in a Bottle.'"

"The Court remains a cloistered institution, perhaps too cloistered, its ranks filled more and more with blindered Ivy League elite. A criticism that has followed the selection of new justices is this: he or she does not have a chance if the applicant was not a member of the secret Yale Skull and Bones Club or the Harvard final clubs, fraternities or sororities.

"There are scores of vitriolic, even hateful, commentaries about every one of the present Court, but actually very few definite threats.

"The problem of strict constitutionalism–if it could really exist–has its proponents and opponents. And that has created an entire other set of Court opponents and even haters. Did the meaning of words used in the Constitution evolve over time? In the last thirty years, entire disparate social cultures have accepted or rejected the proposition. Were any of those oppositions so thwarted as to warrant murder? More than a few persons of interest we talked with thought it was the most likely motive for the murders. Are the justices—individually or in aggregate—too political or too ideological? It is no secret to insiders that the personal calculus of the individual justices is more influential than it should be.

"Are some of them too ideological, too political, or too wrapped up in their personal biases, as to be tolerated any longer? Is the process of appointment too skewed, too eastern, too elitist? Angry people from all sides attest one point of view or the other on those subjects, some with considerable venom.

"The task force formed to carry out the murder investigation exhausted every avenue that they could come up with, all to no avail.

We decided to look into even very unusual possibilities. In the course of the subsequent investigative actions, we ruled out involvement by Islamic terrorists, Chinese, Russian, or other nation state actors, American extremists on the right and the left; and still we could not find a plausible motive, let alone get good information leading to the identification and apprehension of perpetrators. In answer to the questions posed earlier, the response is no. We failed to find enough antipathy towards the court by any individual or group to consider a criminal investigation into them.

"The already murky situation was made much worse by new calamities; seemingly involving barely related individuals—Court interns Greta van der Brakel and Claire Jackson, then finally, Senior Associate Justice, Mr. Angus Dagon Zysteric.

"Into that milieu of confusion and disappointment finally came a break from an unlikely source and from a motive none of us had thus far entertained. The informant was a person living and functioning in the world of international criminals. He proffered factual information with evidence that the motive was an old fashioned one: plain old greed.

To make this story come to an end despite all the grey areas encountered, we then obtained proof positive that a cabal of a major private group of billionaires–criminal conspirators–was responsible for the murders. The reason was to cause the United States to become debilitated with doubt about itself, to doubt whether or not this case could, or even should be solved. There is evidence that they even planned to manipulate the great nations—the US, China, Russia, and even the Middle-East countries—to suffer attacks that would be misconstrued as to source that they would do the unthinkable; make war, and involve allies to turn their war into a new world war.

The criminal conspiracists looked forward to such a war to open new arms, drugs, and to create shortages, that those billionaires could find previously unimagined profits. Crime and enrichment of crime lords flourishes in chaos.

"The Chinese have recently arrested a large number of individuals, joined into what is a consortium which functions as a criminal conspiracy. The billionaires charged– and their underlings who carried out the crimes–are all of Chinese extraction, and the People's Republic of China is determined to act sternly and decisively to punish these mega-criminals and to do so with such robust punishments that they will serve as far into the future as anyone can see, as prime bad examples, and hopefully as deterrents.

A note of caution, however. The PRC is unpredictable and largely inscrutable. Right now, it appears that there are two Chinas: Hong Kong and Shanghai. The people of Hong Kong are fighting a courageous battle against very long odds. Meanwhile, people in Shanghai have stepped over that threshold and live well under a Faustian bargain with the CCP. Who knows what will come next?"

"In conclusion, we can still trust the honor and efforts at objectivity and in pursuit of the rule of law of the

Supreme Court and its future. Thank you for this privilege of speaking. God bless and protect the Supreme Court, and God bless America."

Whether or not there was any connection or some unlikely perverse coincidence, the day following McGee's dramatic speech before Congress, he received a visit from the Chief of Detectives of New York City with the explosive statement that he—Joseph, Patrick, Aloysius, Micheal, John, McGee–was the primary suspect in a first degree murder and ordering him to come to One Police Plaza the following day for interrogation. McGee's psychological zenith immediately fell to its nadir.

-THE END-